The Long Sandy Hair of Neftoon Zamora

MICHAEL NESMITH

•

The Long Sandy Hair of Neftoon Zamora

A NOVEL

St. Martin's Press ☙ New York

Design by Ellen R. Sasahara

Library of Congress Cataloging-in-Publication Data

Nesmith, Michael.
    The long sandy hair of Neftoon Zamora: a novel / Michael
Nesmith.——1st ed.
      p.   cm.
    ISBN 0–312–19296–7
    I. Title.
PS3564.E78L66   1998
813'.54——dc21   98–19510

First Edition: November 1998

10 9 8 7 6 5 4 3 2 1

For Neffie

The legend is the soul emerging into form, a singing soul which not only carries hope but which contains a promise and fulfillment.

—HENRY MILLER

The Long Sandy Hair of Neftoon Zamora

1

ERE LET ME SET DOWN A TALE OF NEFTOON ZAMORA.
Somewhere in the southwestern United States, in a region
unclear on the maps of its generations, there is said to exist
a town named Chuchen. Those who suppose, suppose it only
fancy, fluttering and sweeping with the sands in the desert
wind, but those who know, those who have been there,
place it in New Mexico, south of Gallup and north of Lords-
burg, somewhere along the Continental Divide. I traveled
there in search of the town and Neftoon Zamora and found
what I thought were signs of the city, but I was never sure:
only a few relics among some of the locales entwined in my
own adventure. But the exact declinations of the town are
not important. What is important is what happens there in
certain times and its effect on our lives.

I first heard of Neftoon Zamora in the late 1900s, in the
spring of the year. I was south of New Orleans, in one of
the outlying swamps, visiting Doc and Aileen. Doc lived in
the swamp in a house built on stilts with little more than a
few sticks of furniture, a generator which he connected to
a blender he used for margaritas, and his books, thousands
of them.

He was a medical doctor, a neurosurgeon, but had re-
tired from what he called the barbarism of his practice. He
had become convinced healing could come about some other
way than by cutting people open and manipulating lumps of

their flesh. He was one of the wisest men I knew, so whenever I traveled anywhere near his home I made the effort to see him and Aileen. Aileen was his pet alligator.

I never knew what to expect from him, but through the years his words and thoughts had had a profound effect on my thinking and how I viewed life. So, on this visit I listened with great interest as he told of Neftoon Zamora.

His tone was reverential and he deferred his wisdom to Zamora's. Doc told me Neftoon Zamora had lived among the Indians in New Mexico for a time and was venerated by them as chief or high priest because of a heroic act, the details of which he was not certain.

The legend of Zamora's advent was most strange. According to the stories, he was part Zuni, part Martian, and part Delta blues player and had come from the Great Spirit, Mars, or some place in Mississippi, thousands of years ago. It was the Delta blues part that captured my immediate interest, though it turned out this was the least of it.

Doc said he had a recording of Neftoon Zamora singing some of these blues, rummaged around, produced an audio cassette, and played it.

For those unacquainted with the blues, it is not necessary to know much except all blues sound essentially the same. What counts is the individuality of the singer, the soul of the performer. Everyone plays the same three or four chords; the melodies are almost indistinguishable, so the captivating part is what the player brings to the form. In the presence of a rare and gifted player or singer, one can capture for a moment a special feeling. It may cause you to cry or laugh. Sometimes it can change your life. It is this essence that compels everyone who hears the blues to listen to more. That is what riveted me to the music of Neftoon Zamora that day.

The sound was ordinary enough, the words unremarkable, but the soul of Neftoon Zamora was indescribable. It crept into my mind like a great truth, ineffable, instructive, uplifting in the way it vaporized the illusion of the material world. I knew I would have to search Zamora out.

I suppose Doc knew this as well, since he took care to give me the very few details he knew of Chuchen. From time to time, most unexpectedly, something like this tape of songs will come into my life and rearrange my priorities. I will drop everything and head off on a search. These are the most exciting times for me, and these adventures require all my balance. Too fast and it's like tearing open the petals of a spring blossom to find the flower and in the process destroying what I was looking for; too slow and the opportunity slips away, closing around me like the sea into the wake of a passing ship. It was a delicate and precise act, this dashing off on an expedition into the unknown. But by this time in my life I was used to these impulses, knew how to pack, when to run and when to walk, when to go and when to stop. This was a time for going.

I listened carefully to Doc's scant instructions, and determined at once to find Chuchen. I said an abrupt thank-you and good-bye, which would have been impolite outside the purview of our friendship and his deep understanding of the force that was upon me. Just as I was about to drive away Doc held up his hand to stop me, reached into his pocket, took out the tape, and tossed it to me. I had forgotten it. He shook his head in a knowing way. "Just remember," he said, "the New Mexico license plate says 'Land of Enchantment' right above the number. A Dios."

I drove all day and into the night until I came to the small town of Quemado in New Mexico. At the café there I asked for directions to Chuchen. The man next to me, a Zuni I think, began to chuckle.

"Son, you've been tricked," he said. "Chuchen is a town Indians tell of when they want to make a fool of a tourist."

I told him I was really looking for Neftoon Zamora and he laughed.

"That's even more of a trick. Neftoon Zamora is an old myth, told by fools to children. Outsiders hear and come looking for him, but he never existed. You are searching for Santa Claus." He winked at the cook behind the counter, got up and left.

In the parking lot I was approached by an old woman selling jewelry. She held up some items and showed me one in particular, a small pendant. She said it had been made by Neftoon Zamora. I couldn't tell if she was serious or not, or whether she had overheard my conversation in the café. I didn't remember seeing her in there.

The pendant was unremarkable and just like many I had seen sold at curio shops. I decided to play along for a bit and asked her to tell me what she knew about Neftoon Zamora.

"Neftoon Zamora was from Chuchen, but Chuchen is gone now. It was east of here, in the mountains, in a place only hikers can get to. It was a small village with no connection to the world. There were maybe a hundred people

4

there once. Neftoon Zamora lived there. She was their chief.''

I shouldn't have been so surprised. I don't think it showed. I thought about the recording and realized the voice was genderless, sometimes low like a man's, sometimes high and lilting like a woman's.

"She was a big woman. Six feet tall. Very handsome. She had long sandy hair that hung to her waist and a beautiful body, hard and powerful. She dressed in many different ways, but most like the Navajo, with a velvet shirt and leather pants and white moccasins. This was the pendant she hung around her neck. It was the only jewelry she wore.''

"Did you ever see her?''

"Yes. Many times,'' the woman said. "She would come from the mountains and visit the children in the towns. But all the people would come to hear her stories. This was in Old Horse Springs. She would tell tales and give the children some of the jewelry she had made. I was one of those children. She has not come for many years now. I last saw her when I was eleven.''

"Have you ever been to Chuchen?'' I asked. "Do you know where it is?''

"No, but there is a man at Apache Creek who knows the way. He is Little Horse. I haven't seen him for years but you can ask anyone there. Whether he is alive, I don't know.''

I bought the pendant, as much for the story as anything else, thanked her, and decided to head to Apache Creek.

In the car I put the tape on and listened again to the voice. It was true. There was little to identify the sex. Sometimes Zamora sounded like a woman and sometimes like a man, though when she sounded like a man she really sounded like a man. But one thing was clear. Whether I was searching for Santa Claus or not, no matter if the old woman was playing me for a fool, someone was singing on that tape, someone who was real, someone who sang with an authority and purpose that springs only from the highest musical spirit.

It was night and I was tired, so when the gas station attendant told me of a gravel road that would cut some time off the trip to Apache Creek, I was grateful. I headed east to Pie Town and turned right onto the road. It would be about twenty-five miles to the next paved road.

The soft night air blew through the car window and the moon turned the sky purple as it rose over distant mesas. In this moonlight I could barely make out the figure of a man walking by the side of the road when he suddenly jumped in front of the car and waved me to a stop.

He was an old black man—how old I didn't realize until I pulled to a stop alongside of him and he stuck his face in the window. He must have been ninety. His hair was snowy white and thin, barely covering his head, and his skin was a blue-black that shimmered in the night. His black eyes laid perfectly against pure white.

"Gimme a ride to the highway?" he asked.

We were on a desolate road, I hadn't seen another traveler since I had been driving, so I couldn't say no. He walked around the car and hopped in, sprightly and agile, the age I saw in his face not seeming to affect his movements or presence of mind.

"I'm looking for the town of Chuchen," I said. "Have you ever heard of it?"

"Oh yeah. The home of Neftoon Zamora."

"That's exactly why I'm looking for Chuchen. What do you know about Neftoon Zamora? What can you tell me?"

"Oh," he said, "I knew Zamora well . . . was a long time ago, though. Been dead, mebbe fity–sisty years now. Only people I know tries to find Chuchen, really lookin' fu Zamora, not the town."

"But you knew him?" I was excited. Something in his casualness rang of truth. I didn't believe the old woman; I did believe him.

"Oh, yeah. See, I growed up in Chuchen . . . well, not all the way up. Left there when I was fifteen. But Zamora come to town, I guess it was when I was around nine or ten. Was a mulatto, black as me but with light skin and long sandy-colored hair. Come from Mis'sipi, tol' me. Got run outta there fu'be'n white. Somebody was white some-where's cause boaf Mom and Dads was black. Chuchen's a lil' town wif lots a different folks, lots a different race. Was even a Chinese guy there. But mostly Eyetalians. They was almost white but, you know, kindly green-like color to 'em. Chuchen been built up from lotta people got run off from they home. When Zamora gots to Chuchen's when the Indians showed up."

"I thought the Indians built Chuchen."

"Nossir, they was the Anasazi built Chuchen. They left when the Eyetalians come in. No, Indians, like, you know, Bombay and Calcutta. You know, from India. They showed right about the time Zamora come in. Lot of them thought Neftoon was Indian too. But I knows that weren't so. Za-mora come from the Delta, tol' me, lil' town on the river called Chotard. Tol' me that anyways. But you know, I never knowed that fu'sure. Wadn' no Indian. Knowed that. Could play music too. A playin' fool. Played music better'n any I heard.''

"I know." I turned on the tape I had in the player. "A friend of mine gave me this. That's why I came here, looking for him."

Zamora's voice rang out over the speakers and drifted out across the desert, over the Chamisas, into the night.

"That's Neftoon all right. You know it. Where'd you get that?''

"A friend. I don't know where he got it."

The old man smiled, obviously pleased.

"I haven't heard that sound for years. Oh, my but don't it sound good. Yeah, that's Zamora singin', playin' too. I remember that old guitar. It was a Silvertone or somethin'. Used to play to us and sing. How many songs you got. I don't remember no recordin'."

"There are thirteen on this tape. I've learned some of them, trying to learn all of them. I'm a musician myself."

We were approaching the paved highway and the old man was leaning forward, peering through the window, as if looking for something on the countryside, when the paved road came into view and he began to shuffle in his seat.

"There. This is where I can get out."

"But . . . can I buy you dinner, or . . ." I was trying to think of some way to get him to tell me more about Neftoon, anything to keep him with me a little longer. "Could you . . . do you know where Chuchen is?"

I stopped the car at the intersection and he opened the door and stepped out into the moonlight.

"Where Chuchen *is*? Hmmm. Cain't get to it by car

anyways. I don't think I could find it mysef. Nossir, not by mysef.''

I took one last leap.

"Neftoon Zamora . . . he was, I mean, he was real. Not like . . . Santa Claus?''

"As real as me. Real as that tape. Real as those songs. Thanks fu' the lift.''

He walked away from the car, down the highway, and was swallowed in the darkness.

I turned onto the highway toward town when waves of emotion began to roll over me, slowly at first, then wave after wave rushing in, somewhere between terror and awe, between sadness and loneliness, flooding the chambers of thought until it seemed I would drown in *tristesse*. I pulled the car to a stop on the side of the road, got out, and stood silently in the night air looking up at the stars. Who was that old man? Where was he from? What was his strange accent?

I leaned against the side of the car and gathered my wits. Up in the sky I saw a shooting star. At first, when I look up into a star field, it always appears static, but after a few moments, when the eddies of thought subside and my field of vision settles into expanse, the sky comes alive and I can sometimes see shooting stars. Watching the night sky for a few minutes, the anxiety faded, and I pondered my search for Zamora.

The word that kept rolling around in my mind was *Spam*. It had many popular uses now in slang but I realized it was more than a word, it is the only real American pâté. A crow flew overhead—was this a sign of good luck? A song sprang to mind. I only remembered some of it but it seemed like a good song. Was there a clue here? Then it all faded and I thought about Spam again, a registered trademark for a food product.

I slipped back into the car and put on the tape of Neftoon Zamora. I wanted to see if his could be popular songs as well, but my heart froze as I listened. The tape had changed. It was a language course, in some unusual dialect and tongue. A woman repeated *smarmy* then said in the new language—*ungerret*—then *smarmy*, then a man said *ungerret*.

Clearly I was being taught an unknown language. I ejected the tape from the player and looked at it. It was the same tape Doc had given me, but now it was different and Neftoon's songs were gone.

All the way out from New Orleans I had listened to the tape and had memorized many of the songs, so I still had them in mind, but the feeling of loss was overwhelming.

It must have been that old man, that old black man with the funny accent who had somehow tampered with my treasured tape and put in this language course. For all I knew that old man could have been Neftoon Zamora himself. At the instant I had that thought another crow flew over—another sign of good luck?

I put the tape back in and listened to more of the language course. The woman said *recalcitrant*, then a long moan followed by a click of the tongue against the hard palate, then *recalcitrant*, then a low moan ending this time with a snap of the fingers. I didn't know whether to follow after the old man or continue on my journey, but it was certain I had been given a message. I was really getting ticked off about losing Neftoon's music. I wanted to continue my quest for Chuchen.

I roared up off of the shoulder, throwing a spray of tiny road gravel and screamed into the night. I began to sing the songs of Neftoon in an effort to drown out the language tape, but the louder I sang the louder the tape would play, even though I never touched the volume control. The woman said *floral*, giggled, and said what sounded like an Arabic number pronounced backwards.

Here, alone with the heartbreak of losing the tape, I became determined to shout down the new tongue. The woman said *ineffable* and then something like *flamella* then *ineffable* then a man said *flamella*.

A crow flew across the path of the car and I smacked into it, a black rag tumbling into the weeds. In my rearview mirror I saw the crow get up and try to fly off. It didn't seem to be doing too well, sort of listing off to one side and drifting into a circle in the sky. If he keeps that up, I thought, he'll end up right where he started.

I was going well over a hundred miles an hour when I saw the lights of town. On the outskirts a billboard, lit by the lights of my car, said WELCOME TO APACHE SPRINGS. A shudder shook my body. Wasn't this supposed to be Apache Creek? Up ahead the lights from an old diner streamed across the road. The sign above it said LITTLE HORSE DINER. The words below it burned into my mind. HOME OF NEFTOON ZAMORA AND THE LOST RELICS OF CHUCHEN. I pulled into the gravel lot and parked next to a jade-green Harley with whitewalls and a sense of purpose. The Harley was beautiful, the chrome shining in the lights of the diner. In the nacelle of the headlight were the words "try our Spamburger" reflected from a sign on the front door of the diner. Had that old man put a spell on me? I went inside.

11

The night air in New Mexico always moves, a restlessness that rolls along the great open spaces and makes even the slightest breeze feel as if it is on its way to somewhere. So when I walked into the diner the stillness was the first thing I noticed. The incandescence of the lights filled the interior with warmth: caressing, and very, very still.

From somewhere in the back, the kitchen I think, appeared a Chinese man. His accent had the ricochet cadence of a Chinese speaking English as a second tongue, but his use of the language was impeccable.

"You can sit anywhere you'd like" he said, dismissing me with this remark and returning to the kitchen.

The diner was spotless, with dark blood-red Naugahyde seat and stool covers bordered in cream piping, the floor checkered with black-and-white vinyl tiles, everything else stainless steel or chrome, even the walls. It was stereotypical, an impossible and perfect replica of something I had seen before in a picture. I sat down at the counter and looked around.

On the counter back, with a menu holster on each side, was a Seeburg remote jukebox station shaped like an old radio in bright chrome, with flip panels inside turned by external tabs to reveal the list of songs. All the songs on the jukebox were by Neftoon Zamora.

In each of the menu holsters was a pamphlet with a different cover. The one in front of me was titled *What Is a Friend?* by Augie Rootliff.

The jukebox was five cents and I reached in my pocket for change. The Chinese man came back out from the kitchen holding a knife, fork, spoon, napkin, and glass of water. He saw me fumbling.

"The jukebox is free. You don't need any money," he said as he put down the setup. He took a menu from the holder and handed it to me.

I didn't look at it but said, "I'll have a cheeseburger, mayo only, fries, and a chocolate shake."

"Oh no. Nothing like that here. Only Moroccan food."

I ordered something wrapped in a leaf and studied the Seeburg. When I pushed the button next to the song "You Got to Trust the Pilot," the Seeburg lit up, clicked, swallowed the command somewhere into its electronics, and the song came over the speakers in the diner as well as from the big, mother-ship jukebox standing in the corner. An orchestra, mostly synthetic, began lush sweeps and someone who sounded like William Shatner began a half-sung, half-spoken recitation of the Zamora tune. I looked at the song list in front of me. It *was* William Shatner, sounding like he did on his recording of "Lucy in the Sky with Diamonds." The song was by Neftoon and the name Neftoon Zamora was listed most prominently, so on first look it appeared that Neftoon was the performing artist. Then I saw, listed below his name, the actual performing artist, William Shatner. Then I saw the others. Clint Eastwood singing "Get Out the World," Leeza Gibbons; Crash Test Dummies; the Cranberries; David Letterman and Garry Shandling in a duet; Hamza el-Din, the oud player; Bobby Sherman; Dan Rather; all of them singing a Neftoon Zamora song. As Shatner proclaimed his way through "Pilot," the Chinese man returned with the food.

"I've never seen or heard of these recordings before," I said as he set the plate down.

"They are the only way I can get the songs in here.

13

Everybody asks for the songs of Neftoon Zamora and these are all I could find.''

I reached in my pocket and produced the cassette with Doc's scribbled handwriting of Neftoon's name. I held it for the Chinese man to see. I thought I saw a faint recognition, something quickly set in his eyes.

''This tape had the songs of Neftoon Zamora on it, sung by Neftoon himself. They were amazing. That was when I left New Orleans, but something happened to them and now it's some, some . . . language course. All the songs I see on this jukebox were on this but . . . I don't know what happened, they're gone. I was playing them in the car for a guy I picked up on the way here from . . .''

''An old nigga?''

I choked and stared at the counter. I had not heard that word in normal conversation for years. For the last few hours I had been driving deeper into the the land of enchantment, it glowing rosier as I went, and now this? Did I hear it right? Were racists allowed in the land of legends and myth?

''That old nigga that wanders around here? He's a thief. I don't know how he does it, but he can steal anything.''

I had to say something.

''If you mean the African-Amer—''

''Oh, bullshit, mister. Don't start that. He's an old nigga man, and it's what he calls himself and what I call him too.''

''You may call him that, and he may call himself *nigger*, but don't say it around me.'' I was edgy, looking him straight in the eye. He returned the stare but with a subtle smile, like some kind of game had started, as if he was unabashed and engaged.

"I didn't say *nigger*, I said *nigga*. There is a difference. *Nigger* with a flat and hard *r*, like you say in Texas, is the pejorative. *Nigga*, ending with *ah* like I say it, is nomenclature. I can spot a racist for miles because of that simple shibboleth. You say *nigger*, I say *nigga*. Big difference."

I blinked. Was he right? Chinese is a language of infinite subtleties. The same word, used for widely different ideas, is changed in meaning by slightly varying inflection. Could this man before me tell intricacies of meaning by the emphasis, inflection, and pronunciation inside a word? I had never noticed the difference until he pointed it out. Was there such a difference? I was confused. Among the short-order fry cooks I had ever met, this was the trickiest, most nimble—even clever. Before I could muster protest, he plowed ahead, moving on, leaving me browbeat.

"But if you want to know his name . . ." he let go a flashbulb smile: on, then just as quick, off; almost like a nervous tic. "It is Jefferson Washington. He was the unfortunate recipient of that equally unfortunate moniker because both his parents were slaves. Whatever his name is he is a thief. I won't let him in here because every time he comes in something is missing when he leaves. The last time he was in here the sign on the wall that said 'plate of shrimp' changed to 'boogie 'till you puke.' "

Shatner had mercifully stopped singing.

"Well," I said, "he must have stolen these songs too. They were certainly there when I left New Orleans and I drove all the way here to try to find the source of them. What does your sign mean outside, 'home of Neftoon Zamora'?"

Another flashbulb smile, then he sized me up for a few

seconds. He looked left, then right, then back to me, and must have known he sent a shock through me with these words.

"Exactly what it says, mister. That's Neftoon Zamora sitting right over there."

He pointed to the end booth. I could see the top of a head, obviously covered with long sandy-colored hair.

The quest, the quest. It ran through my mind as I looked at the booth where Neftoon was sitting. Beginning the second I had heard the tape I had been on a hunt, a search for something. I didn't want it to end yet. Besides, what if Zamora was something less than my fancy and the mystery surrounding him had made him out to be? As I walked slowly toward the booth, more and more of Neftoon Zamora came into sight and I became more and more entranced, then surprised.

She was beautiful. I have thought many times since this encounter about how I would write down what I saw that night and have dreaded the prospect because words fail me. I had never seen such an exquisite, comely presence. She did, indeed, have sandy-colored hair that fell to her waist. As I approached she looked at me through gray-green eyes with a dazzling light behind them. Her features were those of a perfect beauty, not defined, or absolute, but active beauty, the beauty of her time, the beauty of a loved one. Think of the most beautiful person you know. Not that you have ever seen, but that *you* know, right now. That was the beauty of Neftoon Zamora and it settled around me, an atmosphere, a magical, breathtaking loveworthiness.

There was also a courage to her face. I remembered the woman in the parking lot at Quemado describing her as

handsome, and the person before me was certainly that. She
looked directly at me and I felt as if I would faint. The look
contained grace, serenity and a power that shook the night.
Everything I had imagined about Neftoon Zamora was in
that look; all the mystery and wonder, the enchanting tales,
the overpowering sound of those songs Doc had given me,
every impulse that drove me here from New Orleans in
straight flight, was staring back at me through that look;
inviting, embracing. This was Neftoon Zamora, of that I had
no doubt. As I arrived at the table I could see more of her
figure and she was clearly quite tall, over six feet, trim,
wearing a white, Western-cut shirt, jeans, and cowboy
boots. As I walked up she was finishing a solitaire game of
jumping little pegs, arranged in holes on a board, one over
the other until only one was left. She set the board down.

Then words I'll never forget.

"Hey Nez, sit down." She motioned to the seat across
from her while looking me in the eyes. It was as if she knew
me. There was a comfortable, clear connection, old friends
reuniting, friendship intact. She was easy and immediately
intimate, but how did she know my name?

"How do you know my name?" I asked, incredulous.

"I saw you on TV. Didn't I?"

Of course she did. Years earlier I had been on television
and had even made a few videos. Out here I had forgotten.
Out here I was swept up in something enchanted. I wanted
it to be telepathy. It was television.

"The fish eat my furniture?" Neffie asked it as a question. It was a line from one of my videos. I laughed.

"Mine too," I said, and she laughed with me.

I sat down. I instantly liked whoever this was.

"That guy just told me that you're Neftoon Zamora."

"I might as well be," she said. "That's what Li tells everybody. I'm his tourist attraction." She put all the pegs back in the little board and slid it off to the side of the table next to another Augie Rootliff pamphlet, this one called *What is a Child?*

"Well, are . . ."

"There is no Neftoon. Santa Claus. I know everything there is to know about Zamora. Li hires me to come in and sit here and when someone asks about Neftoon Zamora he sends them to me and I spin the legend. Sometimes I say I actually am Zamora when I think I can get away with it."

"So Neftoon is a . . . myth, a, a . . ."

"Folklore. Just folklore. It's a good story, though. I can tell it to you if you want"

My eyes were riveted to this woman, and something deep in my mind, some ancient longing, was rejecting what she was saying, hoping instead she was Zamora, a desire to believe, almost overpowering.

"Yes, I would like that, but actually I have this tape of songs a friend gave me he said was Neftoon Zamora. That was a real person singing. So I . . ."

"I'll bet it's Jefferson's great-grandpa. He used to sing the blues and was supposed to be the best. Do you have the tape?"

I pulled it from my pocket. "Yes, but something has happened to it. The songs are gone and now it's some language course or something."

She took it from me and studied it.

"Really?" she said. "That's odd. Have you got a tape

player in the car? Oh, well, of course you have. Can I listen to this?''

She slid out of the booth and stood up. She was easily six feet tall, more likely six-two or -three. I followed her out of the diner and to the car where she sat down in the passenger seat.

I put the tape in and the language course came on. She laughed at the word *flamella*.

''That sounds like a comedy routine. What happened to the songs?''

''I don't know. After . . . Jefferson got out of the car the songs were gone and this was on it.''

She reached up and hit the direction switch on the tape player and the tape changed sides. The blues of Neftoon Zamora blasted out into the night. I felt like a dope.

''Wrong side,'' she said.

I looked down and then began to laugh again.

''You must have been enchanted. Oooooo. The land of sorcery and magic and an old hitchhiker that stole the songs from your tape. Li could have made a fortune off of you.'' She waved her hands around in the air like she was waving away spirits.

''Is this whole thing that big a scam? What IS your name? Why are you doing this?''

She leaned back in the car seat and listened for a moment to the singer.

''That's definitely Jefferson's great-grandpa. Call me Neffie. If I tell you my real name and Li hears you say it then he'll toss me for sure and I need the job. Have you heard the country songs of Neftoon Zamora?''

I shook my head no.

19

"Those are terrific too. I don't know who did them; sort of a cross between Hank Williams and Gene Autry. Really. It sounds like it would be weird but it's pretty good."

"Santa Claus, huh? Too bad. I was looking forward to digging around the mystical city of Chuchen, sitting at the feet of Neftoon, learning the wisdom of the ancients, hearing some stories and a little blues guitar."

"Let's go back inside." I followed her past the Harley and into the diner again, where she took up the same position in the booth. Li came over.

"You see. Neftoon Zamora in person. Like the sign says. Did she find the songs the old man stole?"

"Yes, I suppose she did."

"You want dessert? I'll bring you something." He walked away before I could answer.

"He'll keep the food coming all night. When you stop eating he'll find something else to sell you."

I wanted to know more about Chuchen and the songs and singer on the tape but it wasn't the same now. I had gotten deeply into the wizardry and wonder, so much that when I started playing the wrong side of the tape I was sure something mysterious was happening. I was enjoying it, but Neffie was final and spoke with such authority I was willing to let go of my fantastic journey. Besides, I was getting interested in Neffie herself.

"So, this is an unusual job you have here. Where are you from? I mean how did . . ."

She looked up and motioned for me to be quiet. Li was approaching with a cup of coffee and a hot piece of apple pie with melted cheddar cheese on the top. He set it down and threw a look to Neffie.

2

$\mathcal{D}$O I HAVE TO TELL YOU, SOME TIME LATER, WHEN I returned to the Little Horse Diner, it was not there? Nothing was left but a concrete pad where the diner stood, the gravel parking lot all but scattered into the ground around it. I say this now under the assumption you know the general drift of contemporary mystical mumbo jumbo and in an effort to avoid any "wow" that would come if I were to tell it to you chronologically. Life is enchanting enough. No one needs to have some mysterious force capriciously over-turning the natural order of things from time to time in order to keep my attention. It's worse if these notions in-culcate some blind faith in miracles that set aside the laws of the universe to reward those who deserve a break in the pandemonium. We all deserve respite from evil, and it is this constant that is worth pursuing towards a permanent, enduring peace.

Let me also tell you how this story ends with the dis-appearance of Neffie, in one of the unspeakably sad chapters of my life. This I will explain as the tale unfolds, but not to the end of surprising you or creating melodrama. Of course, I did not know this as I drove behind her that morning to her house, a small adobe snuggled next to a low hummock and out of sight of the dirt road that led us both there.

She handled the big Harley like a seasoned rider, and when at last we came to her house she rolled to a stop, parked, and dismounted with a flair that convinced me she had been riding all her life.

The house was small, an old adobe probably built sometime in the forties. I sank into the couch in the main room while Neffie went in to a back room. I had not realized how tired I was and almost immediately drifted into a dreaming sleep.

I was in the hills looking out across a vast plain. Behind me I heard a rustling and turned to see a wolf coming from the Ponderosa pine that covered the hills. It was a big she-wolf slowly walking toward me with yellow eyes and a benevolent curiosity. I stood there unafraid as she approached. Wolves have always looked to me like big dogs and I have never felt any fear of them, so I reached out my hand as a gesture of friendship. I say I have no fear of wolves but I have never seen a pack or been the object of a pack's attention and when I saw another wolf appear at the edge of the trees, then another, my heart beat faster. The big female continued her slow approach, never taking her eyes off me as more wolves appeared until there were about fifteen standing in a great circle around me. I held my hand out, still, and when the big wolf got close enough she sniffed the back of my hand, then sniffed the air around us. The other wolves on the edge of the forest began to move toward us when suddenly she turned and through some unseen signal instructed them to stop, which they did in unison.

I reached out to touch the fur of this beautiful creature and began gently stroking her hair in one long sweep from her head to her tail. I was careful not to pat her since I instinctively knew this would be seen as too familiar and condescending. The other wolves turned and walked back into the woods, and as I stood there still stroking the silky fur of this animal, I woke up.

It was getting dark, the last rays of the sun leaving a lingering rose through the small windows of the adobe when, in the half-consciousness of first waking, I saw Neffie, standing by the fireplace, building a fire. She was naked and as the fire began its first yellow glow of life she turned and walked to me and sat on the floor next to the couch, her long beautiful body backlit with the flickering new firelight.

She lay her arm across me and began to rain kisses on my face, caressing my shoulders. As I slid off the couch and into her arms I ran my fingers through her hair, feeling each thick strand throughout its extraordinary length.

I sank into her embrace and into her heart, engulfed in her gentle beauty as our kisses fell onto one another with a mounting intensity, meeting at a point between us we each could see. We stayed wrapped in each other until the day had gone and there was only the halo of moonlight across the room and shadows looming from the fire. We had not spoken a word.

When at last Neffie rolled over and turned to the fire, I fell back into a half-sleep and had the same dream I had before, but this time the big wolf was standing next to me looking across the plains. I sat down on the grass and the wolf did the same while keeping a respectful distance. The contract between us was clear and we needed to do nothing more than be with each other, both gazing across and pondering the great expanse before us in silence, sufficient to only wonder, and be there.

This time Neffie's slight stir brought me instantly awake and I saw her sitting with her knees drawn up to her chin, her arms wrapped around her legs, her hair flowing down her back into rivulets on the floor behind her. She put another log on the fire and the yellow flame and sparks danced around her silhouette, throwing the outline of her fantastic face and figure against the wall.

"If you like I can tell you a legend of Neftoon Zamora."

I nodded and propped myself against the couch, stretching my legs forward so I could stroke the outside of her thigh with my toes.

"This is only one of the legends. It refers to this area and this history and these people. But there are other legends of Zamora that are of different times. I learned them out of curiosity and to keep Li happy. As you can imagine, when the first poor fool came in all pumped full of the land of enchantment and I could say nothing about Zamora, well, it was a heartbroken man that left and a very unhappy Mr. Li who watched a potential customer vanish without buying anything. Anyway, there are several legends of Neftoon Zamora, all of them similar and all of them different. No one agrees on whether Zamora was a man or a woman and whether he or she really existed or is, like you have heard, just Santa Claus. The only agreement I can find is, man or woman, Neftoon had long sand-colored hair that hung below the waist and was worn loose, although sometimes gathered in a band.

"The first sighting of Neftoon Zamora was thousands of years ago, before the Anasazi, before any record of any people in this territory. This was a time of the most brutal and inhumane existence for man. There were not many people, and what few there were huddled together in small bands— you couldn't call them tribes because they had no social order. I say they huddled together because that's what they did. Man was not the master of the plains. He was prey.

"The rulers of the plains and all the territories around were the wolves. Now, these were not the breed you see today. They were enormous. The average size was over three feet tall at the shoulder and around one hundred and fifty pounds and they roamed in packs of fifty or sixty—or more. Each pack had a certain area it hunted. They were not scavengers as they are now, and they were very territorial. Sometimes wars would break out between these packs and reduce the size of them, but these wars were always fought to a stalemate, so it would not be long before things would return to normal. You may have heard wolves are monogamous and mate for life, but not these wolves. They were more like wild horses with one dominant male in a pack and many females he protected and sired children with. These dominant males were warlike and the cause of the trouble when it started.

"So, man was constantly in fear for his life and the wolf his greatest enemy. These people were also different than the people of today. They were small—a big male was a little under five feet tall—and they were stupid, having lived so long in fear that all they thought of was basic survival, running in terror at the slightest sign of anything off-key. From the stories, I gather they lived in a small region to the south and stayed mostly in the cliffs and caves of the mesas, coming to the plains only for water.

"These forays for water were dangerous and only a few members of the huddle, as I have come to call them, would go. Here the wolves would stalk them, and if the humans made the mistake of going two days in a row at the same time, or if the wind was wrong, they were almost certain to die. The living conditions in the caves were wretched, but because man had prehensile hands and feet and the opposing thumb, he could climb to these cliffs and the wolves couldn't. So, while it was a wretched captivity for him, at least man was safe.

"Then, as the story goes, something even more terrible began to happen with the wolves. Somewhere along the line a giant male was born, and when he had matured was over two hundred pounds, standing almost four and a half feet tall at the shoulder. He fought and killed many of the other wolves and took over their packs one by one until he had over two hundred wolves in his pack and under his control. There was another wolf, the smartest of all, who had a pack nearly as big and between the two of them they controlled all the wolves in that small but all-inclusive world. Finally these two met in combat. This fight has a legend of its own, but suffice it to say, the big wolf was victorious and so consolidated all the wolves under his control, even the males that were born. Did I mention his fur was black? It was. Coal-black and shiny. The only spot of color was his yellow eyes ringed with gray. In the legend he is known as Black Wolf.

"Our pitiful humans by this time had dwindled to no more than a few dozen pathetic people grouped in twos and threes, not in any families, but randomly, wherever they happened to find themselves in the evenings when they would seek some cave to crawl in before the sun went down. They lived on wild berries and roots and had no central activities other than sex and watching for wolves. Except for one thing. Sometime in their past they had learned to make clay, so clay pots. This one skill was their protector, because it allowed them to live in the cliffs away from the springs and lakes, carrying the water in these clay pots up to the caves.

"It was into this sorry state that one day Neftoon Zamora came. The legend is vague on how she got there. You'll forgive me if I tell the tale with Neftoon as a woman, but that is how she lives in my mind. So, one day she appeared at the doorway of a cave. By all reports she was immense, but it is hard to tell how big, since, as I say, the people were so small that anything over five feet would seem huge to them. Nonetheless, the accounts have her towering, with her head in the tops of the trees and such, so clearly her height was impressive. And, as always, the long sandy hair.

"Along with her height, she was strong, able to pick up a full-grown wolf, hold it over her head and throw it high enough so it would die from the fall when it landed, and she was fleet, able to run down a wolf.

"Many stories converge here. It is told how she showed the humans to use clay to make bricks, and how to arrange bricks to form walls to create barriers to keep out predators. Here they could sleep, live close to the source of water, and safely keep their children. She showed them how to use a tree laid against these walls to climb over them to safety and then pull the tree in behind them, thus making themselves secure.

"She also showed them how to build a fire with flint-rock sparks and dry prairie grass and she showed them many other foods from the land, including the baby cactus.

"Black Wolf watched all this progress from atop his mesa, and the more he saw the greater grew his concern because he knew that the knowledge man was gaining was making him more secure and no longer a source of food. Black Wolf also could see the day coming when man might rule the land and the wolf as well, and this was the most disturbing to him. He resolved to do something about it: Kill Neftoon Zamora.

"Zamora, of course, had encountered this type of hatred before, and knew to never let Black Wolf out of her sight. She always watched him, as he paced back and forth along the edge of the distant mesa of his home. And even though Black Wolf's plans for Neftoon's destruction were palpable, Neftoon was so powerful she could handily win a confrontation with any single wolf, so she was not afraid of him alone. The only worry she had was of the pack, and because she was aware of Black Wolf's scheming, she was on guard for any sign he might try to mobilize the pack against her.

"But it was not Black Wolf she had come to conquer, it was the miserable ignorance of the people. The simple protection from the wild that she taught them took immense amounts of patience on her part, so paralyzed with fear were these people. They also had a small history they called on, full of old superstitions and politics that obscured the enlightened ideas she offered. It was months before the people came down from the cliffs and slept in the first dwelling Zamora built for them.

"You cannot imagine what it was like when she showed them fire for the first time. They all ran screaming back to the dwellings and huddled together for days until one ventured out for lack of water and saw the fire contained, providing heat and light.

"So it went, Zamora with her advanced ideas and desire

32

to help, the people resisting her because of their entrenched stupidity and old ways, and Black Wolf pacing, menacing, waiting. Had it not been for one particularly good student the whole story would have come to nothing.

"There was a young boy who seemed to know intuitively the goodness and progress Zamora was bringing. Even though he was ostracized as a madman for it, he followed Zamora wherever she went and would fearlessly try many of her ideas. It was he who helped Zamora build the first shelter, he who harangued the tribe to try things out, and it was he who helped her watch for the wolves.

"As you may imagine, many years later, after Zamora had gone, he became their leader and went from being thought a fool who endangered the tribe to being venerated as the wisest among them, the one they turned to in crisis.

"I told you they had clay pots. These pots were a reddish color because so was the color of the ground in that territory. One day, when Zamora and her faithful student had gone to the river to get some water, they had taken many of these pots with them. It was late summer and the blackberries were ripe, so Zamora picked a few to eat on their journey. When they got to the spring, Neftoon broke a branch from a green willow tree and chewed the end of it until the fibers made a brush. Then she mashed the few uneaten berries into a dark and beautiful ink into which she dipped the brush, and as her student watched transfixed, she painted a careful line around the rim of the pot. Next, she added a series of dots below the line and finally another line below the dots. She showed this simple design to her friend and he broke into a smile that lit the heavens. Keep in mind that this man had never seen anything like this, a design that

33

did nothing but beautify the pot, and to see Zamora do this spontaneously was to him to see the face of God.

"Of course, that is exactly what it was. What manner of thought was this Zamora had exercised in the midst of the most terrible existence, except to give these people a glimpse of the higher idea, a sense of beauty that made no sense, loveliness for no reason other than its own loveliness. In that moment of recognition Zamora's student touched the idea of infinity. This was Zamora's real purpose in coming, and she thought at this instant she had succeeded. At least, that is what she thought for a few seconds. Because then, the boy took the brush from her, dipped it in the ink, picked up the pot and made the most grotesque scribble imaginable. And try as he might he could do little more than make horrid little scratches on the pot until at last he tossed it away in a rage. The pot shattered into a million pieces against a river rock.

"For the next few weeks Zamora tried to teach the boy this art, but it was of no use. The pots she painted seemed to garner no interest from the rest of the tribe and sat in a pile with the rest, undistinguished. After a while the student refused to paint, even though he would, with the same attention, watch her paint, but it was little more than a curiosity to him.

"Then one day, when they went for water, her young friend brought a reed instead of a willow branch for Neftoon to make into a brush. The reed was hollow and brittle, so even though she could not make this type of stick into a brush, she said she would show him something else. Next to the water was a sharp granite rock stuck deep into the ground with only an edge showing, and Zamora took the reed and sawed it back and forth until she had cut a small wedge from one side. Then, using another more pointed rock, she punched holes along the stem. She blew into the end and a shrill whistle came out, rising and falling in pitch when she covered the holes with her fingers. I can tell you Zamora is no musician, but the noise the crude little flute made had an effect on the young boy that was far greater than the first time he saw the design on the pot. Zamora continued making little bleats and noises from the flute, when the boy reached out and took it and immediately made the most beautiful music. This time it was Zamora who was transfixed.

"With no training, no influence, no history to trace to an origin, the music burst forth in melodies. This new noise drifted across the plain to the dwellings of the people, and this time, instead of being afraid, they were overjoyed, and rushed from their houses to the spring, single file, making a long serpentine line that wandered through the fields of waving grass, running to this sound and gathering around the boy, swaying and moving their feet in rapture unconfined.

"Far away, on the mesa top, Black Wolf saw this exuberant procession and a final fear gripped his heart, for he knew this was the beginning of the end of his wild, and if he was to protect it, and prevail, he would have to make his move.

"The celebration at the river continued unabated throughout the afternoon, and as the day progressed, the young boy played better and better until, at evening, the music he piped flowed from him in great waves, like outbound ripples of a rock cast into a still, deep, pool, spreading slowly from its center to an unseen shore. If Zamora's designs on the pottery were the face of God, this was surely the voice.

"The sun was beginning to set when the boy stopped his playing. As each member of the tribe picked up a pot full of water and set off to their little village, the young boy came to Zamora and stood before her, grateful, obliged to her with an unpayable debt, a debt that Zamora canceled with a caress of her hand across his cheek. Then, standing by her side, he looked up at the mesa where the wolves lived. Together they watched Black Wolf surveying this little group heading to their home. As Zamora and the boy stood there, each was filled with an ineffable sorrow, knowing the one would never see the other again beyond that sunset.

"Zamora took the back of his hand in hers, and unfolding her fist like a blossom into his palm, gave the player a handful of dried blackberry seeds she had culled from the ink she made, letting them fall into his hand before using both her hands to wrap his fingers tight around the bounty.

" 'If you put these in the ground, pour water on them, and tend to them for a season, they will grow into a plant with berries and you will have food.'

"The boy nodded his understanding, then walked away after the others, never looking back, leaving Neftoon alone with the wolves assembling now under the leadership of Black Wolf.

"Neftoon could see the small figures in the distance as the wolves poured down from the mesa into the plain, coming to defend their sacred wild. She knew the only way for the people to be safe was for her to somehow lead these wolves away and destroy them forever. She had no particular plan but decided to walk towards her enemy, to meet them eyes to eyes.

"Black Wolf never lost sight of Neftoon and watched her as she began to move toward him. This was strange. He had always depended on his foe running, had counted on the panic, the fear of confrontation, the terrifying prospect of death at the hand of the pack. This enemy was different. Very well, thought Black Wolf, if she is coming to me instead of running away then I will see to it she gets what she seeks. He trotted confidently down a path on the side of the mesa and took up position in front of the five hundred wolves now at his command. Zamora continued to head straight for him.

"All the wolves spread out in a great half-circle in front of Zamora and came to a stop. With unspoken communication each wolf, aware of the other's position, waited as the circle took shape. Black Wolf reached the apex of this arc and stood, waiting, as Zamora walked toward him, relentless and resolute. He was sure she would stop at the outer rim of the great half-circle, for to proceed further would mean the pack could close in behind her, surround her, and then her death would be certain. Zamora would come no farther than the diameter line between the wolves stationed at the outposts of this terrible embrace, of this he was sure.

"The little tribe, back at their settlement, had gathered at the edge of the enclave to watch, certain as well that Zamora would not proceed to a certain death inside the pincers of the huge pack's waiting menace.

"But when Zamora came to this line she did not falter but persisted, pressing step after step deeper into the center of the pack's control. The lesser members of the pack, confused by this, looked to Black Wolf for instruction. Black Wolf waited. He suspected a trick but he knew that the farther Neftoon came the harder it would be for any plan to work. Whatever ruse she tried would get swallowed up in the sheer size and speed of the pack. He waited and waited. Then, when Zamora had over one hundred wolves to each side of and behind her, Black Wolf bolted, and with him five hundred wolves, each on its separate tack, fangs bared and yellow eyes narrowed, raced toward Neftoon Zamora, surrounded on all sides.

"At this same instant Zamora started her run. Slowly at first, a light jog, but directly toward Black Wolf, a fast-approaching figure stretched low and long in a galloping, ferocious run. Then, she ran a little faster, picking up speed with each stride until she was at full gallop, inhaling and exhaling with every step, her powerful legs hurling her forward at unimaginable speed.

"Black Wolf and Neftoon Zamora, on a collision course, now could see each other's face. Black Wolf showed his terrible fangs, glistening with saliva, etched in white against his black throat. Neftoon leveled her eyes into his, as her mouth drew a thin line across her face.

"They were only a few feet apart now. Black Wolf, swiftest of the pack, ahead of the closing circle of death, strained forward, ready to throw himself into the conflict, when suddenly Zamora bounded into the air, over the head of Black Wolf, who sprang up on his hind legs and snapped his huge jaws together under her. But they closed on air for she was instantly behind him. Black Wolf spun about and gave chase as Zamora leapt above each of the wolves that had been following him, landing behind each, as they too would spin and race after her, mad with anger and frustration.

"Black Wolf soon outran his pack, once again ahead of them all, leading them in outrage, and blind, aggressive hatred after her.

"Neftoon checked over her shoulder to see him only her shadow's length behind, closing much faster than the others. She did not want him too far in front of the rest, and she slowed her pace slightly as she loped up the side of the great mesa that was the wolves' home. Black Wolf was almost within reach of her, but as he was about to jump, she gave an extra burst of speed and pulled ahead. The entire pack was swarming up the mesa now in enormous wriggling lines, giant snakes slithering up the mesa side.

"On the high mesa plain, far above the valley where she had come to pull a struggling people from their fear, Zamora veered sharply, heading away from the little plains and meadows below, to the back side, the cliff-side, of the mesa, to a sheer drop, hundreds of feet to a gaunt, rock-strewn desert, and once again she slowed. This time Black Wolf was on her with a mighty leap, throwing himself so all the force of his forelegs rammed into her back and circled round her neck. But she did not fall. No, to his great and horrified surprise she grabbed his paws with one hand and clamped them together, crushing them as she bound him to her like a sack thrown over her shoulder. With the other hand she reached around and grabbed his jaws and slammed them shut, holding them with a power so great Black Wolf knew he had no chance of escape.

"Then she slowed even more, darting a look back to see

39

the rest of the pack at her heals. Before her was the cliff, and with no hesitation she threw herself over it, holding Black Wolf in her death grip. And, as she had planned, the rest of the wolves followed, all five hundred in wave after wave, falling from the top of the mesa to the desert below and their death.

"All was quiet in the village. Everyone but the young flute player was confused by what had happened. They had no way of understanding this type of sacrifice—no context, no point of reference—so they stood there, mute, perplexed. They knew only that Nefloon Zamora was gone and with her the wolves. It was this legend they told and still tell of how Zamora destroyed the wolves and made the land safe. Our young student knew something more had happened, something much more important and lasting. But because he had no words for it, he too stood there silent."

In firelight from the dying embers, Neffie stood up and walked to the back room, her lithe shadow undulating across the walls of the adobe. I stared at the coals of the fire, contemplating this lovely story, when, after a moment, Neffie returned, dressed in buckskin pants, high white-fringed moccasins with silver conches, a dark-burgundy velvet blouse draped with strands of turquoise nuggets on silver threads, magnificently beautiful. Saying nothing, she sat beside me.

There was a light knock on the door.

" 'S'open," she said.

I turned to face the door and in walked a young black man, twenty-seven or twenty-eight years old, handsome, casual, and obviously at home. I recognized him. It was Jefferson Washington.

3

WHEN CHILDREN DRAW PICTURES OF PEOPLE, THEY DO not populate the eyes. There is a charm to this, especially if the picture contains the usual abandon of the very young. As the artist matures, however, these lifeless eyes become disturbing, as in the case of statuary, where the half-orbed stone in the eye socket creates a mask that covers any real identity, leaving only the body to represent the man. For it is the eyes that are the melody of soul, the eyes that great artists strive to capture, and it was the eyes that let me know the man standing in the door was Jefferson Washington.

When I had seen him on the highway he was old, withered, with a quality of aged wisdom. Here, in Neffie's house, with the gentle susurrus of the wind from the open door and the faint firelight dancing about the room, I saw a young man, vital, urgent. The body had changed. The eyes were the same.

"Li says Kweethu called. Another seeker in Quemado. He didn't buy the gizmo." There was no trace of the old man's odd half-old-time Southern, half-Pakistani accent. He looked at me. "Li's pissed too. He saw you two drive away together."

Neffie walked over to him and bussed him lightly on each cheek.

"Say hello to Nez. Nez, this is Harouk Akeem Ali . . . a.k.a. Jefferson Washington the fifth."

Harouk nodded graciously. I even detected a little warmth. I nodded back.

"Li can relax. I have my own life," she continued.

"He wants us in there in an hour or two just in case. Kweethu said this guy was driving slow, kind of lost. Earl gave him the Pie Town shortcut but he still hasn't left Quemado. He's driven through there now three times, with the tape playing really loud."

Harouk stopped his train of thought, caught by surprise, and stared at Neffie, as if seeing her for the first time.

"Say. You're in the full rig tonight. I haven't seen that in a while."

My mind was racing. It was hard to accept the size of the scam these two were talking about.

"I was inspired." Neffie looked at me and smiled but I did not smile back. I was discountenanced, feeling a slow and steady anger rising, a free-floating anger, aimed at no one, no thing as yet.

As humans we are so desperate to make sense of the insensible we forget the cautions of science and reason. To hear of this elaborate ruse compounded my disappointment at losing the magical tale I was constructing about the origins of the music and the legends of Neftoon Zamora. Disappointment was turning into anger.

Harouk said to Neffie, "Can you give me a ride to six-oh-two?"

Neffie nodded but continued to look at me. She knew something was wrong. She was waiting for me to say something.

"Is this whole thing really that big a con? Is all this really that . . . I mean, are you running a . . . a . . ." I ran out of words.

Neffie and Harouk looked at each other, communicating silently. Harouk was waiting for Neffie, obviously looking for a clue about how much to say.

Finally Neffie said, "Well, yes and no."

There was another silence. Neffie and Harouk once more looked to each other. A decision was being made. They had more they could tell, more than what they had allowed me to know already, but it was taking some consideration on their part. Then they decided something. Neffie gave Harouk a slight nod, went back to the fire and sat down as he settled into an easy chair next to her.

He spoke to Neffie. "We don't have much time." Then he turned to me.

"I'm from Mississippi. Chotard. On the river. Pretty place, the river, the Delta lands, if you know what to look for. I'm fifth generation. The tape you have is my great-great-grandfather. He made the recordings in Chicago in 1929 when he was in his seventies or eighties. They are Delta blues songs like a lot of people sang then, except for one thing. My daddy told me his great-grandpa learned them from his daddy, who learned them from Neftoon Zamora. That part is true. The Little Horse Diner and this enterprise Li has set up . . . well, it isn't what it seems, that is certain. But the reason Neffie and I are here is the legend of Zamora."

He paused, looked again at Neffie. She gave him another slight nod.

"I met Li in San Francisco a few years ago. He was running a gay nightclub called the Blue Parrot, like in *Cas-*

ablanca. I was in there one night with some friends and for some reason had the tape with me and asked Li to play it over the big disco sound system he had. The place came to a stop. About half the people left, the rest listened hard. No one talked, no one danced. They listened. After it was over someone asked me about the tape and I told them the story my dad had told me. They were all swept away by the legend. Li watched all this and that night after closing asked me to tell him more. We struck up a friendship, and I won't go into all the details of how we got here, but we did. Li thought he could make some big play from this, make a lot of money somehow. He sold the club and set up the Little Horse Diner. That's the main part of it.''

Something didn't seem right. I had many questions.

"I have to get up to the road," Harouk said. "If you'll drive me, I'll tell you more."

The three of us left the house, Neffie jumping astride her great green Harley and heading for the diner, and Harouk and me in the car.

"Take me back to the dirt road where you found me." As he talked he reached into a bag he was carrying and pulled out a wig of wispy gray hair and put it on. It was almost absurd in its amateurishness and I felt foolish for not seeing through such a poor disguise.

"Can it possibly be Li has invested all this time and money and effort to trick people into buying more Moroccan food than they want? I can't see the payoff in all this," I said.

Harouk was now in his wig and began the shuffling, bizarre accent from nowhere.

"Well suh, see, Mr. Li he sells mo an'mo stuff. Gots some jewry and things that can cost plenny, yoo know. Folks comes by 'n' pendin' on whose they is can git mighty hung up on Neftoon things."

"What *is* that accent? It's, you know, it's weird. Not like . . ."

Harouk spoke normally. "I know. I know. It's something I made up. I can't keep it consistent. Sort of a cross between Gandhi and George Foreman and the old man Richard Pryor used to do as part of his act. It fooled you, though."

"Confused me more than anything. Really . . . how does the payoff work?"

"When people are on a quest you can sell them almost anything. Doesn't make much difference what the quest is, as long as it takes them over. Born-again Christians. New age crystals. Astrology. Quantum physics. Li set up a system to qualify people, and then if it looks like they are ripe for Zamora lore he feeds it to them in more and more expensive packages. One guy dropped half a million dollars on a ring. Another paid a couple hundred thousand for a pot. Like that."

"Harouk! That's big-time criminal stuff! You guys could . . ."

"No, no, no. Nobody tells any lies. Nobody tricks or defrauds anybody. These people are here looking on their own and seeing what they want to see. Li simply charges them for it. The only part that is unbelievable is that they pay."

"You're in a costume. Li told me 'That's Neftoon Zamora, over there.' I mean, of course you're telling lies."

45

We had come to 602, the gravel road where I had first seen Harouk.

"Here we are. Let me out here. I'll walk up the road."

"But if this guy doesn't come . . . ?"

Harouk reached into his bag and showed me a cellular phone. The car rolled to a stop.

"I'll call. Those were not lies that cost you anything. They were part of the atmosphere. Part of the staging. When it comes down to it, there is nothing illegal going on."

Suddenly his phone rang. Harouk flipped open the talk panel and spoke in a low voice so I could not hear. Then he closed the phone.

"This guy is still in Quemado. You mind waiting here for a bit? Gives me somewhere to sit."

"You are creating an atmosphere of deceit. Maybe it isn't illegal but it's unethical, immoral. You're stealing trust."

"I won't argue with you about that. I'm getting ready to move on, anyway. See my folkses knows that when I comes out here that I be back and theys be waitin' . . . besides, I'm fed up with Li. I thought he was okay, but he's a racist pig like everybody else. I was happy in Mississippi until I found out I was gay. It's one thing to be black in this country. Try being black and queer. I ran for my life. Li seemed easygoing, not . . . you know, like, like a . . . I mean, he ran a gay bar, for god's sakes. But when we got out here the real colors came through. I'm going to New Orleans. It's hard there too, but I'll be rid of Li."

With the motor off, I could hear the night as it rolled in. The crickets with their low *burrups* and the irresolute wind singing through the wire fences laid the background sounds at the feet of the sky. The two of us sat there staring through the windshield at the tableau of mesas and stars, at the plains with their yuccas spread out singularly, like tombstones; at a small independent cloud as it bruised the moon, occluded it, then moved on. Harouk flipped the visor down, looked in the mirror on the back of it and primped the tatty wig. His head wagged back and forth, his eyes towards the mirror.

"You know, Harouk, I don't know which interests me more. The story of this outrageous scam, or what you said about your grandfather learning those songs from Neftoon Zamora."

"I can tell you which is the most interesting. It's Zamora."

"So, tell me."

"The tapes were made from some old wax records I found around the house. We didn't have anyway to play them, so they were just kept around. Mom and Dad treated them like treasure, which they were, and so while I never knew what was on them I always figured they were special. When I went off to school I kept thinking about them and met a guy who said he could make a tape from them without hurting them in any way. When I first heard them I was . . . I can't describe it. It was like hearing some basic sound, like a heartbeat or the ocean. It was comforting and inspiring and . . . well . . . it was like home. Mom and Dad cried, but I think it was from nostalgia for Grandpa more than anything else."

"Where did you go to school?"

"Started at LSU. Went there for two years. Hated it.

Then transferred to UT at Austin and finished up there. Degree in business, of all things.''

"You're very lucky."

"You mean 'cause I'm black? Maybe, but Southern rural living is different from urban living. I missed a lot of problems. Strong family. Dad was good, a real friend, sold farm supplies. Grain. Hay. Seed. Fencing. So I did fine. Missed the plight of the black man. Didn't miss the rage. Got that plenty. Assholes like Li.''

"So . . . Zamora."

"Yeah, well, it was the sound of the earth and the wind and everything basic. And there was this wail, this cry to it like something from outside the world, somewhere in the stars. I asked Dad if he had ever heard these songs before and he said once, when he was young. He has this blues collection like a white man and listens to the blues all the time, but he stays away from clubs and such, doesn't smoke or drink, goes to church, AME Zion. What can I say? Sort of distances himself from them. Me, on the other hand, I want to sing the blues, sing these songs of my people and live like, you know, Elmore James or Muddy Waters or, or . . . I get taken over by them. Which is very unpopular now with people my age. Blues? Not today . . . too old and forgotten. Problem is, I can't sing.''

"Yeah, well, that would be a problem," I said.

"Dad told me he had heard the songs and that started him liking the blues, and then he told me about Neftoon Zamora. He said it was a legend his dad had heard from his dad and so on, and it was Neftoon Zamora that taught my great-great to sing and play.

"My great-great-great-grandfather was an African slave.

I mean by that he was a slave in Africa. Slavery was in general practice throughout Africa. One tribe would raid another and steal the children and the women and make them slaves. My people were Bantu and lived in west Africa, south of the Sahara in a kingdom roughly where Nigeria is now, in a town called Wukari.

"The people of this land were warlike and fought constantly, but this particular village was supposed to have been peaceful. My great-great-great-grandfather's African name was Aku, and he was stolen from there when he was eleven and put into slavery by a nearby tribe.

"Aku had a sister who was taken from him and sent to another village, so he was alone. He was a slave with this one tribe for three years, when the king decided to take the slaves he had captured and trade them to the Europeans.

"The story goes that when Aku was being carried down the river to be traded he saw Neftoon Zamora for the first time. Aku had been raised in a dusty land where there were only little pools of water, but cleanliness was vital to the culture. They used perfumes made from trees that grew there and were quite careful with their daily habits, making sure the village was kept immaculate. The tribe that captured him was filthy and cared nothing for hygiene. They also lived on a river and used boats to go back and forth to the African coast. Aku had never seen a boat or so much water and was terrified when they tied him up and put him in the canoe. On the first night of the trip all of these strange new things came together and Aku's fright turned to hysteria. Zamora supposedly came suddenly from the surrounding jungle and confronted the native chief who was Aku's captor. Zamora was a big man, over seven feet tall, and was lighter-skinned

49

than the Bantu, more the yellowish tan of the Bushman, and . . . he had this long sandy hair that hung to his waist. Apparently, this scared the hell out of everybody in the trading party. Zamora made the king agree to allow the slaves he had captured to perform the rituals of cleanliness so important to them and that way the slaves became less afraid and a little less miserable. Zamora then went to Aku and told him he would come see him again and not to be afraid. Why Zamora didn't make the king let them go, I can't tell you. But, that's the way the story goes.

"Aku was sold to an English sailor and, to make a long story short, after a few more sales was finally traded to a poor family in Louisiana. I don't want to start on the horrors of slavery, but I can tell you there were three types of slaves. The city slave: These were up in Maryland and Virginia, to the south of the Mason-Dixon line. These slaves were status symbols and were treated well, given good food and good clothes and sort of shown-off like a fancy car or furniture or pets are today. Then there were the country slaves: These were the farm laborers and the cotton pickers and ones that usually were part of the workforce of a big plantation. Then there were the slaves to the poor folks, mostly in the country, mostly tenant farmers: White trash with slaves. This was easily the worst situation a slave could be in. Usually there were two or three in a household and that was where Aku ended up.

"One day came word of a new arrival. A big man with long sandy hair. People began to tell of his exploits. How he stood up to inequity and would refuse to work without compensation. All of which I figure for nonsense. A slave who refused to work was usually beaten to death. What rang true in the stories, though, was the wisdom of Zamora and the force of his fearsome presence, especially to the white man. Aku was interested in meeting this man because he remembered well his benefactor from Africa.

"Aku finally met Zamora and swore it was the same man he saw in Africa. They became friends and through Zamora's teaching Aku learned to read and write . . . and most important he learned to play the harmonica. Aku had been trying out various instruments in an effort to capture some of the music he remembered, but most of the instruments, the guitar and the piano, were not tuned around the five-note scales of his native music. Zamora showed Aku how to play the harmonica in a way so the five-tone scale was easily playable and Aku spent many hours with his 'mouth organ,' as it was called, reliving and remembering the songs of his youth.

"One day, when there was a guitar player and piano player playing with Aku, Zamora took the harmonica and showed them something that changed the face of music forever. Instead of playing a harmonica tuned to the same key the guitar and piano player were playing in, Zamora began to play a harmonica tuned to a different key. We know what it is now, but then, no sound had ever been heard like it. While the other two players played a simple chord progression in C, Zamora played along with a harmonica in the key of F. When they played in G, he played a C harmonica. And so on through every key.

"This kind of playing created a tension between the two instruments and made the major keys sound almost minor, like the third and the seventh of a major scale somehow played flat but not quite. When the guitar player and piano player heard this they began to mimic this strange new scale with their instruments, and the music broke out.

"What all this boils down to is the blues. This 'cross harp,' as Dad called this type of harmonica playing, was the beginning of the blues.

"As you also know it was the root of all rock and roll, which became the most popular music in the world.

"Aku taught this harmonica style to his son and it was his son who made the recordings in Chicago you are listening to on the tape your friend gave you."

"How did he get them?" I wondered.

"When Li decided to set up the Little Horse we made about a hundred copies of the tape and sent them around, left them around, gave them to strangers . . . like that. Like seeds. Just to see what would come up. It doesn't take long or take much to get a legend going. Remember the story about how so-and-so was supposed to have died from eating Pop Rocks, or how you can catch birds by giving them uncooked rice and then water so they swell up and can't fly? People tell each other this stuff and the next thing you know it's part of some universal truth. Same with the tapes. Say a few words about Neftoon, play the tape, mutate that a few times through a few different friends of friends and presto! People start showing up in Quemado looking for Neftoon Zamora and the magical city of Chuchen."

Harouk's phone twittered. He answered by saying "Yes?" and then said nothing else until he closed the connection.

"Well, Nez. Time to go. Li really is a bastard, you know. I guess I'll see you later."

He jumped from the car without waiting for me to say

4

SECONDS LATER I HEARD THE ROAR OF AN AUTOMOBILE engine and then saw a state police cruiser blast past the window, lights flashing but siren off. The presence of this second official vehicle on an emergency call was enough to draw the cowboy pool players outside, where they gathered in a semicircle, bouncing the rubber heels of their pool cues against the wooden sidewalk and watching the disappearing cars twist up the road and into the hills.

By the time I got to the front of the café and stood there with them, only the glow of the emergency lights was visible, still stabbing the night, pools of red-and-blue exploding across the countryside.

"Must be heading up to Reserve," one of the cowboys said.

"Nope. Apache Creek." The woman had come from the café, wiping her hands on her apron. "Somebody's been shot. Heard it on the scanner."

The night was still. The prodromes had come and gone like a paper cut, slicing through the serenity in a second, holding everyone's attention for a second, and would be forgotten in a second, except as a mild nuisance. Up and down the street of the small town, people standing in the doorways and on the side of the road dismissed the two heralds of calamity with a shake of their heads and went about their business.

Except for me. All I could think about was Neffie and her safety. My stomach clenched inside me.

"Probably Mexicans," another cowboy offered. The others nodded and grunted in agreement as they all shambled back inside the Blue Front.

I heard another sound, approaching from the direction the ambulance had taken. It was a low roar at a steady pace, then louder and louder until it was a low roar with the high crackling clatter that could only be the sound of a Harley-Davidson. Coming around the bend in the road at the edge of town, I saw a single headlight. Before the café, the rider slowed and made a left turn and drove up a small paved road. I could see by the glow of the streetlight it was Neffie, her long hair in a braid behind her.

I started to call out but I knew she wouldn't hear me, so I ran to my car and drove after her.

The road she had taken led back into the hills behind Glenwood, winding along the edge of a tortuous creek lined with gnarled trees. I could see the flare of her lights against the cottonwoods as I raced to catch her, and after a few moments I saw the bike itself. I flashed my lights to signal her to stop. Instead she picked up speed.

I had known she was a seasoned rider from watching her before. You can tell by little things when someone has an easy familiarity with riding. With Neffie, it was the way she dismounted, the way she turned the bike around in the parking lot, the way she put her feet on the pegs instantly as the bike started to roll; all the habits of confidence. But none of that prepared me for what I saw now. She was a brilliant rider, a gifted rider, almost a supernatural rider.

She flung the bike from corner to corner and picked up

speed with every turn. Big Harleys are clumsy and cannot respond quickly to rider input, yet it seemed as if she was on the most nimble of sport motorcycles. She leaned so far into the corners that the foot pegs scraped the asphalt, leaving long trails of golden sparks. Even though I began to drive as fast as I could, little by little she pulled away until she was out of sight. I had no intention of abandoning the chase, but I slowed and decided to wait out the trip, to see where it might take me. The roads out here are long but usually go only one place.

After a mile or so I saw a sign announcing the entrance to Catwalk National Park and the road narrowed a bit. Up ahead I saw Neffie's Harley parked next to a grove of cactus. A chain was across the road farther up. I stopped beside the bike and got out. All was quiet. Neffie was not there.

The Catwalk, as the locals call it, runs along the side of Whitewater Canyon, a deep-box canyon that was a hideout for Billy the Kid, Butch Cassidy, and Geronimo, but that is not why it is famous. It is famous because of a water pipe. In the 1800s the canyon was the site of the Graham silver mine. A creek that ran down the middle of the canyon was the source of power for this mine. After the mine was in operation for a few years it was decided to tap this creek and run a four-inch pipe down the canyon to bring drinking water to the town. The construction of the pipe turned out to be a huge project, since the canyon walls were steep, in some cases rising a hundred feet above the creek bed, with sheer rock facings and nowhere to walk. After much trouble the pipe was finally built, but to maintain it, the crews had to walk like tightwire walkers up this pipeline. Not only was there no net, the shards of boulders littered the canyon floor like so many knives awaiting the hapless fall. The pipeline was increased in size to eighteen inches as the town grew, and finally a catwalk was built high along the sides of the canyon walls for the service of this last pipe. The mine was closed in the early 1900s, but the catwalk was shored up by the park service and is now a stop for tourists.

Of course I didn't know any of this as I stood in the night air by the motorcycle, listening to silence, staring up at the shadows of the creek's canyon.

Then, a flash. Neffie's necklace of silver and turquoise and the silver conches on her moccasins shone in the moonlight as she ran up the catwalk, visible only for a second until she turned a corner. I called out but she didn't hear me.

I jumped over the chain across the road, raced to the catwalk and sped up it, calling out her name. The catwalk runs for about a mile into the canyon, up a steady climb of several hundred feet in elevation, and then comes to a stop at a landing that hovers fifty feet above the canyon floor. From there I could see the plains above, but the path that went beyond the catwalk ran out in a few feet, dead-ending into a cliff face.

Again I saw a flash in the moonlight and Neffie far ahead, a small figure on the plains. She was running at an incredible speed, her long hair bouncing behind her like the mane of a show horse. I called again and this time she slowed but did not stop. She seemed uncertain whether she had heard a call or not, then began to run again, fast.

Once more I called and once more she slowed, looked behind her and almost came to a stop, slowing to a calculated walk. I gave the loudest yell I could muster as she disappeared over the horizon. I waited, hoping I would see her silhouette reappear over the rim, but she did not return.

I looked for any kind of path she might have followed but saw nothing. I didn't want to lose her but I was puffing, in a sweat from the run, every muscle aching from exertion. I rested for a second or two then crawled over the edge of the railing at the end of the catwalk and followed the path to the end. Up above and ahead I could see a ledge jutting out from the cliff facing. It looked navigable if I could climb to it.

I am not a climber and did not like the prospect of getting up this face, but it was only ten or twelve feet to the ledge. The cliffside leaned away from me a few degrees so it was not a vertical ascent. I stuffed my fingers into a crack in the wall, lifted myself up and secured a toehold. From there, at the limit of my reach, I was able to get a grip along the side of the ledge and pull myself up the rest of the way. Once I was on the ledge I had barely enough room to stand if I kept my back to the wall. I stood up.

This was a mistake. I looked out and down. I was seventy-five feet up but it felt like a thousand. Below me the water slammed onto a boulder and sprayed plumes into the air in great arcs. Then it fell down into a pool made by other boulders, rushed through the cracks between them and continued its journey. The force of the water was inconceivable, the roar an awful groan from the rocks beneath the foment. This was no little creek. I felt as if I was on the side of a blender, looking down at the blades.

My head spun and I squatted down. It was then I realized I could not retreat. The way up would not work as a way down. I turned in tiny shifts to face the cliff, then began a slow sideways shuffle along the ledge. The path got a bit wider as I sidled along and after a few feet was wide enough for me to walk facing forward. I took a few more steps, then this path came to an end. Above it, another ledge.

The next climb was not so steep. The cliff leaned away from me now at an angle great enough for me to get a purchase with my feet. There was a plant, a little bush, growing from the rocks, so I grabbed it and hauled myself up. I needed one more step to get onto the ledge. I swung my foot up, placed it on top of the bush, grabbed the ledge above and gave a great heave.

In one terrifying split second my foot slid off the bush and instead of hoisting me up, left me hanging by my fingertips. I clung with all my strength, but the effort was not enough. I did not have the grip to sustain the weight of my body, and as I pulled, my fingers slipped and I began to fall. I reached out in a frantic dive to stop at the lower ledge but there was nothing to grab and I bounced off the ledge and began to tumble, faster and faster, down the cliffside.

A tree was growing out of the cliff and in desperation I lunged at it but only caught a few branches, which broke off in my hand with the force of the fall. It slowed—but could not halt—the downward plunge. I hit a small uneven crevice in the rock with my shoulder and the jolt shook through me with a numbing, buzzing sensation. Upside down now I careened into the wall, its surface a razor-sharp abrasive, tearing the skin away from my arm and elbows. I reached out, my arms over my head toward the platform of rock rushing up at me, but my attempt to soften the impact was hopeless and I smashed onto the rock, my head curling under my body, my chin driving into my chest as the shock of the fall pushed through me. My legs arched over the top of my head and I landed on my back, feeling the small rocks below me crack ribs as they punctured the skin.

I lay still, dazed, barely conscious, only aware I could not breathe. A howl came out of my mouth, a cry from the traumatized lungs and I lay there wailing, until slowly, in short inspirations, the breath returned.

I looked at the night sky and for a moment could not remember where or who I was. I tried to get myself to a sitting position but my forearm was fractured and would not brace me, so I rolled over on my side and put the other arm under me and lifted myself up. I felt a trickle of blood down my back at the same time as blood dripped into my eyes, partially blinding me.

I was lying on a small platform made by an intersection of boulders, still twenty feet above the creek. I could not raise myself all the way up with my arm so I tried to slide my feet under me. As I pulled one foot toward my body, my arm began shaking, then gave way. To my horror I rolled off the platform and fell again, this time with no ability to resist.

I struck the side of the huge boulders as I went headlong, a blow to the side of my head flipping me over and tearing the skin from my cheek before I arrowed feet first into the fierce creek, where my legs buckled and snapped like toothpicks.

Consciousness was ebbing. Crippled with pain, blind from the blood in my eyes, limbs broken and useless, I had no way left to fight. The pull of the stream came as a great deliverance from the enormity of the fall. I sank into the water after my broken legs and felt the bubbles and the

foam in my shredded ears and mouth, covering me in darkness, holding me down, down where there was no life, no
breath, only a gaping void, a maw.

I felt my shirt tug around me, hung on something, pulling me. Then another pull around my broken collarbone.
Then my arm was seized, held by some power, and I felt
sure the shoulder was going to come out of its socket. Another somersault under the crush of the water as I rolled
over and felt a pressure across my chest, a band of power
underneath me, lifting, pressing on the shattered rib cage. I
was coming out of the water, I was above the water. I could
breathe. I was lifted up into the sky, the clear night dusted
with stars. Higher into the stars and the sky and the great
rocks on each side of the canyon walls, up, up, until I was
still. I was held still, gently, on the quiet shore of the creek
on a small patch of sandy earth that smelled of patchouli and
rain and sandalwood.

More blood ran into my eyes and her hand wiped it
away and brushed my hair from my face. I looked up into
Neffie's eyes, she looked down at me. I saw the muscles
flex in her powerful arms and hands as she cradled me for
a moment before laying me down onto the sand. She had
heard me and returned to me and saved me; embraced me,
in her might as much as her mansuetude.

In the quiet, I hear "Telstar" by the Tornadoes. A satellite, *Sputnik*, whizzes by, dangling from an invisible string,
like something out of an old Flash Gordon serial—no wait,
like Captain Video or maybe it was Buck Rogers. The embers from the rocket fire fall down and out of frame in the
gravity of the times, the sparks rise with the smoke like
fireflies and wander back and forth, serpentine, like the pat-

terns on the entrance to a Parisian subway, and "Telstar" seizes the drifting, rising smoke and shimmers a little inside a Fender Super Reverb guitar amp, inside the Mississippi magic of the blues guitar, but it is not inside, it is outside, in outer space, and the chords are changing and changing and changing, not the usual one four five four five. There is a guitar, it is four in the morning, a maroon plastic flip-top Admiral radio (with a handle so they can call it a portable) leans up against the wall and plays the top 40 on a humid Saturday on the outskirts of Dallas, Texas; hot, so hot there is no escape. "Telstar" swings by and disappears into space again going the other way across the frame and my little universe, the universe of my house, my mom, my dog Buttercup, stumbles into the open and I see the background of their being, the ocean and the sequence of waves, incident, reflection, coincident. I hear a theremin and Xavier Cugat. I hear "Frenesi."

I am in a shopping center next to the Country Club Pharmacy where they pound the hamburgers so thin they cook in five or six seconds and the broccoli turns olive-gray from being on the steam table for so long. I'm outside the CCP and walk down the sidewalk in front of the grilles of the artfully parked cars with the 1957 chrome smiles, chrome bullets, chrome rockets, targets, handles, mirrors, portholes, twin antennae, and there is a music store with records and pianos and organs. He is in the window.

The moths dot the glass, shuddering, wriggling in ecstasy and misery, trying to get through the plate glass, and I am with them. He is in the window playing the organ, the big Hammond or Conn or Wurlitzer, sitting on the bench that juts out from the console like a military jaw, sitting over a bank of pedals arrayed like a row of teeth, playing them with his feet. "Perfidia." Latin sounds. He rocks back and forth, shaking his shoulders, Cugat in big puffy sleeves. Two rows of keyboards and his staggered hands cross and uncross to find the keys and there is a warble from the Leslie speaker cabinet because inside the Leslie the speakers are mounted on rotating platforms so they spin when he switches them on and the sound warbles, like a bird. "Cherry Pink and Apple Blossom White." I can't believe it. Hands and feet dance around the big grin of the organ and this, this . . . sound comes out. I stand there as the neon comes over the night and turns us red. I see my reflection. There is a hole in my pants. As I walked towards the music I dragged the hand shoved in my pocket along the Arizona flagstone walls to feel the buzz through the material, the rub; sensuous, like a vibrator, too young and stupid to know it would wear a hole in my pants. I feel foolish.

He is playing and I see his thinking and know he is thinking this up somehow but cannot imagine how he is doing it, turning his thinking into these sounds. "Telstar" comes around again and the sounds are the same. Then, from far away, the blues. Then Jimmy Reed and Lightnin' Hopkins and Hank Williams and Jerry Lee and Chuck. The Mighty Chuck who takes all the rhythm and pounds it into the lyric pound for pound for Ezra Pound. "Poetry is language charged with meaning." I can't move. There is pain.

Both my legs and my arm are in splints. The walls are white adobe walls and Neffie is sitting over me. Next to her is a man with long, sandy hair like hers but thick with gray. He is old, very old. They look at each other and Neffie lays her hand across my forehead, looks at me, says something I can't understand, something to comfort me. Only the spirit of the remark cools her hand and my head. A light comes through the doorway and outside I can see the sky, cerise and cyan, see the brighter stars of last night, a line of vermilion etched along the top of distant verdure giving way to the yellow of a morning sun, then "Telstar" plays and *Sputnik* flashes by again.

"Can you hear me?" she asked.

I thought for a moment. I nodded yes.

The old man came to the bedside and stood beside Neffie.

"You will be well soon. This will pass quickly," he said.

She is blond and blue-eyed and we are kissing in the front seat of the car, on the brown-wool seat covers, and I can feel myself getting hotter and hotter, so hot there is no escape, until she pushes me away. She is walking home and carrying her schoolbooks across her chest, her arms wrapped around them. Why does she carry her books that way? She giggles. I rest them on the bone, she says, on the natural shelf I have down there. She is not embarrassed but curious about my reaction. My reaction is "what bone?" but I say nothing. The Corvette is red-and-white and I'm shaking so bad because I know if she can just see me in it, see me just once, she will think it is all okay, that I am all okay, and she won't push me away again. I know it's the car. The old car with the terrible-sounding motor and the brown seat covers that are wool and so hot in the summer, so hot there's no escape, so hot. She is carrying her books and I come to a stop and offer her a ride but she must know I have gotten it from a car lot, that I have lied to the salesman and taken it for a test ride. She knows it will always be the hot wool seats and the musty smell of the old car, the torn headliner. She walks on and I see the smiling grilles of the new cars beaming in the lot outside the store where the man plays the organ and fills the night air with the sounds of "Telstar."

"Telstar" by the Tornadoes. A slap and a swish, the sound rushes by, *Sputnik*, beep, beep, beep, RKO Radio Pictures lightning bolts in the black-and-white silver nitrate void of space with gravity, the gravity of the times. Got me run, hide, hide, run, anyway you want me, to roll. Yeah, yeah, yea-u-h-h.

Anything for a convertible. I know it's the car. A turquoise-and-white '57 Chevy convertible with fender skirts and a lowering kit because my friend's mom and my friend can see the fire in the belly and let me have my way and I like him and he likes me. The root beer that comes in a frozen mug from the drive-in wipes off of the Naugahyde interior with a simple sweep of the rag. In the brown wool of the old green two-door it sinks down and stays wet and gets sticky until it dries in a hard encrustation, testifying to the lurching out-of-control idiotic transmission. The Chevy has Powerglide and the root beer just wipes up with a rag while the twin exhaust pipes make a little thunder with the Mighty Chuck as the road rolls underneath the car. It is his convertible and there is nothing I can do but take pictures and send them to the girls on *American Bandstand* and tell them I will give them a ride in my car when they come to town, nothing I can do but ride in the passenger seat and wave at her, inviting, offering her a ride in a car without the sticky-sweet stains of the root beer because it wipes off so easily. But it is his car. It is not my car.

Old Spice and Vitalis with V7 in the white two-door Bel Air hardtop with the small block, with the big boys. Drinking and counting the hours till the day comes when school is over. Blue jeans rolled up above the loafers or pulled down over the boots bounce on the twill loops of turquoise cotton carpets over the transmission hump. I want to paint the wheels white. If we could only afford whitewalls. If I could just buy good wheels. I know it's the car. It must be the car.

As I looked down across the bed I saw two aspen posts and the splints on both legs. The light was either half-up or half-down but I could see about the room. A chair in the corner made of aspen limbs, tile floor, an electric lamp on a table, a window to the outside. I couldn't move but did not feel much pain. Then a popping sound coming from within. The bones in my legs and arm and chest were shifting, popping into place. I was uncomfortable but the relief was greater as each bone seemed to set itself. I saw Neffie walk in the room. The old man was with her. They stopped at the doorway and watched for a moment. Neffie looked at the old man, who nodded his affirmation as she walked toward me.

The natural light faded, leaving only the lamp. Neffie and the old man left the room and stood outside the door. I could see past them to other houses set along a cliff wall, adobes, lit from inside with the same electric glow the lamp in my room was giving off, a faint yellow with a slight tint of pink. The houses, six stories of them, stretched away, beyond my view. Neffie and the old man embraced lightly and went separate ways. From somewhere far away I heard music, the sound of an electric blues guitar played by a

master. The sound wafted in and out of the room like a
breeze, sometimes louder, then softer.

I tried to move my arm but could not. None of the
fingers on my right hand would articulate.

A radio sits in the fake-wood dashboard inches away from
the brown wool and I'm sitting on the floor and feel the
brittle bark of the old carpet like jute against my legs. The
bass is pounding and there's a vibration like the vibration of
my hand moving along the Arizona flagstone outside of the
Country Club Pharmacy on the way to the smiling organ
and the man who would be Cugat. And the vibration is new,
exciting, sexy, and it is thunder and power from the center
of the earth to the center of the heavens. I listen louder as
Carl Perkins and Jerry Lee and the Mighty Chuck thump
and crash and scream along, blowing down the back wall at
light speed across the South. From the Delta it is a shout
and a holler and a threat that encircles me and casts me
about like a cork on the ocean, bobbing and bouncing,
twitching and turning into the blues. A thump with no re-
prieve but a simple command from the Mighty Chuck. A
mandate. Johnny B. Goode!

Now there are snakes tied in a ball and rolling around
on the bed with me and they are one body and one head
but many minds and they are biting me on the legs and my
arms and neck, then they are smoke, diaphanous, transmuting into the swell of strings and Mantovani on a stereo in
the store window, into the cafeteria, into the line, into me
standing next to the cutest girl in school—hell, the cutest
girl in the world. She is in the line waiting for the food,
wondering how she looks, waiting and hoping to be a cheer-
leader so she can get all the attention she deserves and I can

smell her dress and the starch in her petticoats and her hair pulled straight back off her tan scalp into blond blue-eyed perfect Aryan twinkles as she takes out her barrette from the ponytail and scratches her name in the hood of my car. Her name on the hood of my car as an insult, the poor old paint on the tired old car that would be a convertible for me but has nothing to use, nothing left to do it with. She is there sitting next to me on the passenger seat and as we round the corner I reach over and open the door and the centrifugal force makes her slide out and tumble along the gravel on the side of the road where her petticoats mash and twist and slide and crush under her while the barrette falls out of her hair onto the road, skittering into the ditch, lost. She won't be scratching her name with that any more. She stands up and yells at me, and me and the Mighty Chuck laugh and laugh and listen to the rhythm of the lyric as it pounds out the last word. "You done started back doin' the things you use to do."

In the South, in the Delta, the songs are free and they rise up and take me with them. But I am not the South. I am the Texas blues, brown-wool seat covers that soak up the root beer and leave a sticky stain. I am white and poor and hot and humid. I cannot make a fist now. I cannot make a fist so I listen to the band and the band closes each finger down around the brass knuckle, around the roll of quarters, and thumps the big speaker next to my ear as I lie pounding out the rhythm with my new fist on the floorboard of the car until my mother can come out of the house where she has gone to deliver the artwork. The artwork for layout. The layout for the advertisement. The advertisement for the bank. The bank where there is no credit for a single woman.

Not for new tires. Not for whitewalls. Not for anything. The thumping pulsing Arizona flagstone buzzing bass lines lie against the side of the wall outside the organ store. I smile back at the great chrome car gods in their stalls, at their diamond teeth and whitewalls, and hear the smear of the Mighty Chuck and Hooker's Boogie Chillun and I know I will have the car. I will have the smell of the dress. I will fold it all into the downtown punch and tumble and trouble of the fifties and sixties and rock and roll as "Telstar" flashes by, as the Tornadoes play, as the organ warbles. The man in the window is me. The man in the window is calling, singing Texas blues. Texas country. Cugat pudding. You got to trust the pilot when you get on the plane. I feel my legs and arms; the music from far away does not fade but gets louder. There is more light. I am falling down, slipping from sultry sleep, suddenly awake, down to earth, here, now.

I tried to sit up and to my surprise found I could raise myself up on my elbows although my legs still seemed immobile. I wiggled my fingers a little and rolled my head around my shoulders, relieving the pain in my neck. Then I felt a slight trembling in the bed and a low and distant hum came into the room. I looked out through the doorway and thought I saw the sky move, like looking out of a moving train. No. More like looking out of a great airship as it lifted into the sky.

5

I STOOD BY THE EDGE OF MY BED AND WATCHED THE stars outside the door shift in the sky and, with no conscious thought to do it, found myself at the front door, looking out. Outside the door was a sleeping porch the length of the apartment, where Neffie was asleep on a low single bed below the sill of the screens that surrounded the porch, and beyond I saw the earth slip away as the city, once set into the canyon side, slowly lifted and rose into the night sky, like a hot air balloon.

I felt a tug on my arm and looked over at Neffie, who was standing by me now and had wrapped her arm into mine.

"We're flying," I said.

She looked at me curiously and said nothing for a moment. Then she looked out the door and back to me.

"Flying?"

I looked out the door again and all was normal. What had been exhilarating a second ago was now terrifying. I was sure I had seen the whole town lift off from the ground. Now it was obviously not so. Was I losing my mind?

"It looked like we were flying, like the city had lifted into the sky and was moving up into the stars."

"Well then, it's landed," she said.

This remark so drew me to Neffie that I stared at her, awestruck with adoration. She could have said so many things, things like "There, there, you must be feeling a little weak from your accident" or "are you crazy?" or even "yeah, right," but she said, "it's landed." She said this because of the abiding respect and love she had native to her, a grace accepting all around her on whatever terms they presented themselves. Not only was the remark supremely loving, it was also supremely confident, secure. Neffie came into my heart and feelings the way the songs on the tape had come into my musical soul, unexpected and inspiring. Then I felt the pain in my legs.

It was not the kind of gnawing pain you would expect from broken bones—more a gentle ache, like a sore muscle from exercise—but I wanted to sit down. I made my way to the bed Neffie had been sleeping on and sat on the edge. Neffie sat next to me.

Outside the sun was rising and the day fast approaching. I could see the city clearly now, if a city it was. We were set at the topmost level of a staircase of dwellings. In each direction the city stretched for about a quarter of a mile, built against the western side of a north-south canyon wall. The city was a series of conterminous apartments, the largest along the bottom row and the smallest along the top, all connected by a series of stairs and walkways along the outer edges. Everything seemed to be made of adobe, but was not in the usual run-down and dusty state of old adobe houses. There was a newness and well-built quality to this structure, giving it a solid, almost rocklike nature. The windows began to shine with bits of light from electric lamps turned in on many of the apartments, chasing away the remnant darkness of the night. People coming out of the apartments began traveling up and down the steps and along the walkways, greeting each other familiarly, quietly, with nods and the occasional brush of hand upon hand.

I noticed the similarity of the people to Neffie. These were not typical of the native American. That beautiful copper skin and shiny black hair were nowhere present. Instead the people were all tall, with light- and dark-tanned skin, and most of them had light-colored hair, in varying lengths and styles. The most striking feature of these people was their eyes, almond-shaped, slightly Oriental, in the most vivid colors. Blue-green, gray with dark-gray outlines, vivid dark-blues, piercing emeralds and purple sapphires. I recognized one of the people walking toward us as the man that had sat by my bedside during one of the preceding nights.

He came to the doorway and Neffie stood up. He had long hair, mostly gray now, but once the color of Neffie's, sandy white.

"He's up," he said, looking at me as he came in through the door.

"This is LittleHorse," Neffie said.

I tried to stand and found I could with little pain this time, but the splints on my legs had become cumbersome. LittleHorse steadied me.

"Welcome to Welach," he said, pronouncing it *Way-lock*. "You came in the hard way."

"Thank you for all your help. I'm sorry to have stumbled in so . . ."

"We don't get many visitors." He turned to Neffie. "There's a dance tonight. Be sure and bring him." Then to me: "You will really enjoy it."

He kissed Neffie on the cheek and walked out.

"My dad," she said.

"Your dad?"

"I know, I know. I have two tiers of defense against unwitting intrusion. I never thought you would make it up here. First tier—the whole Zamora routine Li was running, and second tier—'I'm a regular girl with an odd background.' Most of it was true: Geneva, the modeling, college, UNM—not New York—except . . . LittleHorse is Pops."

There was a thrill in all of this to me, the constant shifting reality, the discovery almost by the second of new things. I felt an unusual trust, and even though Neffie was telling me yet another explanation of her background, I did not feel misled. I felt as if I was being told more, the more I was being found trustworthy.

"And . . . what is this place?"

"Welach." She spelled it for me. "Anasazi word for *city set on the side of the canyon that's really hard to find and be careful you don't fall.*"

She was deadpan.

"Getouttahere," I said after a beat.

"I don't know what it means. *Welach*, I guess, means the same thing as Denver or Miami except we don't have an NFL franchise to give us a media identity."

"Is this an old place, or . . . you know, it looks a little like Taos, or like the Gila cliff dwellings with electricity."

"It's quite old. It's also wonderful. I lived here until I was fifteen or so."

"Or so?"

"No birth records. No city hall—well, maybe Delilah's."

I straightened up a little on the bed. I was feeling quite

good. I stretched out my right hand and wiggled my fingers. Everything was working fine.

"But the state . . ."

"They don't know we're here. Don't know about us at all."

I stared.

"I know it's hard to believe, but Welach has been here for thousands of years. Only a few of the Anasazi knew about it and none of the white settlers ever found it. A lot of the Indians know but they don't tell. The closest was Billy the Kid, who hid out close to here and drew all the cops and press around. But nobody made it back up in here. Recently we've been getting a few high-tech hikers. Every two or three years one will wander into the lot outside of town where we keep some cars, but they never make it all the way back in here. Too hard. Usually one or two of us will scare them off of 'private Indian land.' You can't find this place by looking. Not visible from the satellite spy cameras, not accessible to the average person. Not accessible to the extraordinary person. You want something to eat?"

"Starving."

"Let's go down to Delilah's. Let me see you walk."

I stood up and walked slowly around the room. Except for the splints that kept my knees from bending, I could move fine. The pain was gone.

"Let's take those off," Neffie said, and knelt on the floor beside me as she unwrapped the bandages around the splints.

Finally the sticks fell off and I was free. I bent my knees up and down as I walked around.

"How long have I been here?" I asked.

"Four days. Today's the morning of the fifth."

"Well, I feel great. What's Delilah's?"

"Local hang. Come on."

Neffie took my hand and we walked out the door into a magnificent day. New Mexico skies are crystalline. I always feel as though I can see into outer space in the middle of the day. Usually, like this day, there are tufts of clouds across the blue. All in all a great place to be. This city, Neffie, the day, were making me giddy. I grinned a huge, idiot grin as we walked along.

The pathways along the outside of each level of apartments were about four- or five-feet wide. I could see down to a narrow valley floor and across to the other side of the canyon, which had no buildings. From here it was obvious why the city was not visible from the air. The canyon was a split in a huge plain, so the canyon walls extended down from it, below the plain. Along the top of each side of the walls was a ledge, an overhang of sorts, making it impossible to see into the canyon from above. Even standing on the plain itself one would have to walk almost to the edge of the chasm to be aware of the little canyon; and still, one could not see down into it until standing directly over it. The city was almost underground. In addition, the canyon was closed at each end by what must have once been huge cataracts. I understood how it had stayed hidden all this time.

I looked into the chambers as we passed by. They were simple rooms with simple furnishings. The most remarkable aspect was the art. Wall hangings, vases and pottery, rugs and sculpture. This was not a little town of poor natives but a prosperous, elegant town with inhabitants who obviously valued beauty and order. Yes, *elegance* was the word that came to mind, elegance in the mathematical sense, the simplest and most direct solution to a problem. I wished for a camera, so lovely was all this to see.

"How many people live here?" I asked.

"Maybe six hundred. No one counts, but that seems about right."

"And no one knows about it. You don't pay taxes, don't have government services . . . the things of a . . . you know . . . the economy of a city."

"We have all we need. There aren't many of us here. The town doesn't grow at all. There are plenty of ways we contact the outside, but, no, we are hidden to the world." Neffie and I came to one of the stairs that traversed between walkways and headed down. "When a child is born he or she stays here for the first fifteen years of their lives. Then, even if they leave, they stay close . . . but no one tells. No one from We-lach spends too much time on the outside. It's . . . I don't know . . . crude."

We had come to another apartment, and inside were many people sitting around tables. It was a large room with about fifteen various-sized tables, and several-dozen comfortable chairs set at random. Off to one side was something like a buffet with big coffee urns and some fruit and nuts and yogurt—at least that's what it looked like to me. No one seemed to be having coffee and no one seemed to be doing much eating. They were sitting around the tables and talking, some were writing or studying from books, a few listening to headphones and personal stereos. Altogether very normal, altogether very strange. We walked in and sat at one of the tables. A beautiful lady approached.

"Hi Karen," she said to Neffie.

"This is Nez," Neffie said as she pointed to me.

I smiled and nodded, then said to Neffie, "Karen?"

"The nickname Lisa calls me. Karen LastHorse. What do you want to eat?"

"I don't know. Bacon and eggs, whatever, steak and potatoes, avocado and sprouts, I . . . whatever you got."

"Bring him some enchiladas with rice and beans."

Lisa nodded then said to me, "How do you feel? I hear you took a fall."

"Considering, I feel terrific. Thanks."

"It will only get better," she said, and walked away.

"Karen LastHorse?" I looked at Neffie.

"LittleHorse, LastHorse . . . it's just a goof. We started calling each other that when we were kids. Lisa is not her name either."

"What is?"

"I don't know. Her mom was Cinderella, or something like that, and I . . ."

I suppressed a laugh. The situation was like listening to Shatner sing the blues in the LittleHorse diner. The whole city of Welach was compressing into this unusual space in my mind. It struck me as funny.

"Wait . . . her mom was Cinderella?"

"That's what I called her. I have no idea what her name was. We make up our own name and names for friends, that is if we don't like or can't remember the ones they use. Parents name the kid early, but when the kid wants, the kid changes it."

There was something to this, I thought. I can hardly ever remember the names of people I know casually. Time after time this has kept me from approaching someone I know at a party and saying hello because I can't remember their name, or worse, the name of the person they are with. How great if I could call them anything I wanted and they would accept this. I already did this a little, but only in my mind. I knew a Richard I called Rufus (not to his face since he would not have understood), and a Polly I called Gladys. Don't ask me why; they were names that seem to fit them better. I realized as I sat here with Neffie how regimented and bureaucratic names are. Calling someone's mom Cinderella because that was how she appeared to you was wonderful. What was even more wonderful was that here this practice was considered normal.

"So what did your parents call you?"

"Neftoon Zamora."

I looked into her eyes to see what she was saying. There was a twinkle, but she was serious.

"Really?"

"Yeah. Neftoon Zamora. Now you know. I really am Neftoon Zamora."

"And what did you change your name to when you got older?"

"Miss Twigs and Butterflies."

"Twigs and Butterfl—?"

"No, no, I'm kidding." To my great relief, Neffie laughed. "I didn't change it. I used Neffie. I was named after the legend, the one I told you at Harouk's, which I kind of like. I just left it. I used Miranda Clank when I went to school in the outer world."

The name made me laugh and I started to laugh like a kid. So did Neffie. It felt wonderful.

I remembered, when I was young, forcing laughter because it felt so good. My friends and I would do or say something that made us laugh hard, then we would keep doing or saying it again and again so we could laugh again and again. After a while, of course, the laughter would become hollow and meaningless. To my dismay, I saw this hollow laugh become the only laughter of adults: party laughter, business laughter, approval laughter. The genuine laugh that shook you all the way down was gone, except on occasions so rare as to be countable.

Sitting with Neffie, listening to her tell of the social economy of Welach, I was laughing again for real, laughing with delight, unchained.

As I looked around the room at the other people I felt an unusual sense of belonging. These people did not look like me, were not enthralled as I was, were paying no attention to our table, and yet there was about the room a type of family, a real family, independent of biology or background.

Lisa came back with the food. It looked awful and tasted worse. I didn't keep this fact too well hidden, but Neffie said nothing. She never asked how I liked it. Instead she got up and went to the coffee urns and drew a cup of hot liquid. I thought it was coffee until I took a sip. It was almost undrinkable, a cross between tomato soup and warm vanilla ice cream.

"Not to put too fine a point on it, but this may be the worst food I ever had. What are these enchiladas? They taste like they were made out of tree bark. And the drink is . . . I don't know . . . a kind of melted everything."

"We don't pay too much attention to food."

Neffie never said anything to me about food again, except from time to time, to ask if I was hungry.

"So, on this name thing," I said, "you make up whatever you want to call someone and that works. I mean, what about in a crowd, with people you don't know well . . . you know, if you just make something up, then . . ."

"Try it," she said, pointing to Lisa. "Who does she look like to you?"

I thought for a second. The name Margie came to mind.

"Margie," I said. Neffie nodded, a "go ahead," inclining her head towards Lisa.

I called out. "Margie." Lisa kept on about her business. Once again, louder. "Margie." Nothing. I looked at Neffie. Now what?

"Maybe it's not Margie. Try again. Really think this time. You have to communicate with the name."

"Margie is all I can think of."

"Then, keep trying."

I yelled out, loud, at the top of my voice: *"Hey! Ma-a-rgie!"*

Most of the people turned around, including Lisa, who looked at me for a second, then pointed to herself as if to say "you want me?" I nodded and waved. Everyone who had turned to look went back about their business as Lisa headed over to the table.

"See. That's how it works," Neffie said. There was that twinkle again.

"Neffie, don't be silly. She turned because I yelled. I could have thrown all the dishes on the floor and she would have turned and looked, but that doesn't mean her name is 'broken-dishes-on-the-floor.' "

Lisa was at the table. "Did you want me?"

"I was wondering if you had any way to refreeze this?"

I pointed to the enchiladas, still intact except for the one bite I had taken.

"He wants to call you 'broken-dishes-on-the-floor,' " Neffie said.

"Fine with me," Lisa said as she walked away.

It was clear nobody cared about the food. My jibe had gone unnoticed, even as a joke. The odd part about it all was I was not really hungry anymore. I was not sated as I would be after some extravagant meal, but the one bite I had taken of the mud enchilada and the one drink of the cup of whatever had cured the hunger even if it hadn't filled me up.

I looked toward the entrance to see a big man coming in and heading toward the table. He was dangling some keys from his hand and held them out to Neffie as he sat down at the table.

"Hey," Neffie said. "This is RD," she said to me.

"Artie?" I said.

"RD," he said. Neffie took one set of the keys from him as we shook hands.

"Runs Deep," Neffie said. "RD for short. RD helped carry you out."

"Oh. Thanks," I said.

"You look a lot better now," he said. "We didn't know if you would make it. These are your keys." He held out the other set of keys to me. "I put your car with Neffie's scooter."

RD was tall and handsome with long dark hair, almost black, drawn back into a ponytail. His features were rugged, eyes as clear and black as a moonless summer night, set in a muscular face, model handsome, body like a wedge, with arms the size of some men's legs.

"You coming to the dance tonight?" RD asked Neffie.

"I guess. Depends on Nez." They both looked at me.

"Me? Yeah, sure, I guess. I'd love to see something like that."

"Okay. See you there." RD left, exchanging greetings with some of the people around the room. Neffie stood up.

"Let's go sit on the floor," she said as she grabbed my hand and led me out the door.

The late-morning sun was shining a huge shaft of light through the top of the canyon against the west wall, lighting up all the apartments. All the rest, in light shadow, was warm and beautiful. Neffie took me out to a large grassy area in the middle of the canyon, the canyon floor. I understood the name now. We sat down, she cross-legged and me stretched out. I was feeling good, relaxed and happy.

"What happened that night I saw you racing up to the catwalk?" I asked.

"After you and Harouk left I rode to the diner and took up my position in the back-corner booth where I first saw you. I was sitting there playing IQ when I saw a car pull up and this guy got out, which was fine, except when he went around to the passenger side and opened the door and pulled out Harouk, I knew something was wrong. Harouk was not wearing the wig, and the guy was handling him a little bit, you know, sort of pushing him around. He shoved him in the front door about the same time Li came out from the back.

"Li was nonplussed and seemed to recognize this man. I slunk down in the booth so they couldn't see me.

83

"Li called the guy 'Gus' and started off cool, like he was running into an old acquaintance with bad memories between them. It changed into a shouting session pretty quick.

"Gus wanted to know what Li had done with the money from the center, and Li wanted to know how Gus found him out here. When Harouk tried to get out the door, Gus reached out and grabbed his arm.

"Gus picked up the pamphlets Li keeps around there next to the jukeboxes, you know, that 'what is a wife?' stuff, and started waving it in Li's face and yelling. I couldn't make out what he was saying, but he was mad. Then he took the tape out of his pocket, like the one you got from your doctor friend with the Zamora tunes on it, and he threw it on the counter and really lost his temper. He kept saying 'You owe me, you little chink,' and like that. One time he said he 'wasn't going to take a hit for him' and then another time he said, 'Give me the goddamn money back.' I was only hearing pieces.

"I was trying to figure out how I could get out of there without being seen. There was a little side door about ten feet away from me but I would have to come out and be seen in order to use it. I was thinking I might make a run for it, but before I could decide, everything changed.

"Li was behind the counter and reached down suddenly, which made Gus pull a gun out of his jacket pocket and open fire. Li fell down behind the counter. I can't say for sure he was hit, but I think so. At the same time Harouk broke free and ran out the front door. Gus ran out right in back of him and started shooting. That's when I stood up and looked out the window. I saw Harouk fall, but I think he only stumbled. The bullets Gus was firing were making these little geysers in the gravel and it didn't seem like he was getting too close to Harouk.

"Then Harouk looked up and saw me standing in the window, and that made Gus turn around and see me too. Gus ran back to the front door waving his gun, and I bolted for the side door. I got outside as he came in the front and he fired at me but hit something way across the room. I didn't get the feeling this guy was any good with a gun. I think he hit the Coke dispenser or something because I heard this hiss and saw cola spewing all over the place. I ran around to the front and jumped on the hog. Harouk was gone.

"Just as I got the bike started, Gus came running around the corner and shot at me one more time. This time he hit the front door, blew the Spamburger sign away and the light inside the door. I mean, he was shooting, you know, at a forty-five-degree angle to me. Totally off the target. But it was good for me and I bailed out of there, south. I saw him getting in his car but didn't see him leave the lot.

"After a few miles I saw headlights way behind me. I was sure it was Gus. I was going to go to Welach through the catwalk. About halfway I ran out of gas, of all things, and had to switch over to reserve. When I reached down, the reserve switch was stuck so I pulled off the road and out of sight to unstick it. Whoever was following me came by, and, sure enough, it was Gus.

"By the time I got to Glenwood I was skittish. After I made the turn up to the catwalk I saw the lights from your car racing up in back of me and thought it was Gus. That's why I took off.

"Up in the catwalk I thought I heard someone call but

I wasn't going to stop and find out who. Then when you called out the second or third time I recognized you and doubled back around.

"I was up in back of you when I saw you fall. If I had been there a few seconds earlier I could have either pulled you up or shown you how to get back down. The catwalk is really only for serious climbers. Some of it is impossible. In a way it's good you didn't get any farther the way you were going. You would have gotten into a real jam.

"When I saw you fall I climbed down and pulled you out of the water. I carried you as far as I could but I couldn't get you up over some of the tougher stuff up higher. I had to leave you there while I went back to get RD to help me carry you out. Got you back in here, and here you are."

"Did you ever find out what happened to Li and Harouk and the Fatman?"

"How did you know he was fat?"

"Just doing a movie riff. He was fat, Gus?"

"Yeah, he was. He didn't look like Greenstreet, but definitely overweight, thinking back."

"Excellent. Did you ever find out what happened after you left?"

"No. I've been here with you. Some people have come back from town but they can't get any news. Just another shoot-out. Rumors are some people were killed, but still rumors. I want to go back and check it out. Part of me wants to stay here and leave all that alone, but I'm worried about Harouk. I didn't actually see him leave but he must have been well enough to get out of there."

"I can go in and check it out for you, if you can't leave here."

"Can't? You mean like *Brigadoon*?"

"Well, can't . . . don't want to . . . I mean, if you were still afraid of Greenstreet or something."

"Thanks. No. Nobody will tell you anything anyway. You have to be local. Carry a gun. Eat meat. Wear a hat. But you can go with me. How are you feeling? Can you get around okay? You seem fine."

"Great. No problems. Except for one thing. And it's not a problem, but I . . . I wanted . . . you know . . . I want you to know I am finding myself more and more— what's the word—attached to you. I mean really attached and . . . I have to tell you this because you really are . . . I mean I really think you're . . . you know, really . . ."

I was lost. I had said *really* four times in a row. I was about to say *really very* when I shut up. I had not told someone of my love for them in years; courting had become foreign to me.

Then, horror of horrors, I became embarrassed. But now I had no way to withdraw, to suddenly change tack and pretend I was talking about something else. I began staring at the ground, unable to look up. My face was on fire; I must have been bright red. I thought perhaps if I burst into tears and ran around pretending to have lost my mind, that would cover it up. Maybe I could start singing some old railroad song about death and blood and divert the whole thing with a non sequitur.

Then I stopped thinking in English and strange visions started coming into my head, swirls of color I was sure I could use as proof of insanity. I was insane. That was it, clinically insane from too much fast food. Twinkies. Didn't some killer get away with murder by pleading Twinkies overload? I could also become invisible. Yogis did it all the time. Meditate. Float. Disappear. Something like that. I knew yoga. I could . . . no, wait, the Japanese tea ceremony. Aren't the opening lines of the tea ceremony, "I am finding myself more and more attached to you." You? I mean the tea. Not *you* as another person, but *you* as . . . I mean green tea, green-tea ice cream at the end of a sushi dinner is attached to you . . . but not *you* per se . . . you know, why do they have fortune cookies in a Japanese restaurant? Ever think of that? Maybe that's only in the southern U.S., where Chinese food is all chop suey and egg rolls.

"Me too, Nez. Me too."

Ta-daaa! . . . was all that went through my head. *Ta-daaa!* A fanfare of sorts. An annunciation. Deal closed. Done.

There is no more wonderful state of mind than love. Love itself, being in love, loving, feeling loved and lovely, all work together to create the highest and most happified state of existence. It is love that in one great sweep of the heartstrings brings into harmony the symphony of life, orchestrating and arranging all of life's disparate parts into one grand concord. In love, where the operative word is *in*, like being *in* New York or being *in* a play. True love is a place the lovers occupy, happy citizens of an extraordinary city. Love all around.

This is not love that is physical, though the physical can express it in some minor degree, it is not congenial, courteous, not even convivial, though all these elements contribute some small part to its expression. True love is a type of mutual esteem, a state of shared values and perceptions wherein one's motives turn away from the self, and its constant effort towards satisfaction, towards another and another's world, selflessly seeking another's well-being and happiness, secure that in that simple notion rests all joy.

As I sat with Neffie I was shattered by gratitude. With the broken bones and scarred skin, the recent trauma of a failed effort, of no consequence, I was serene. We sat quietly. Then the kiss.

Neffie's kiss was silent, simple, direct. For that moment, awash in Neffie's being, my heart will sing with gladness for all time. I will never forget sitting on the floor of the magnificent canyon setting of Welach, when my lips touched hers, for in that single act was all the meaning of life to me.

Neffie stood and helped me to my feet. Standing together beneath the canyon walls, below the bank of rising houses to one side and nature's profusion on the other, in the warmth of a noonday sun shining across the floor, in open view and plain sight, we embraced once more, a proclamation to all who would see it, a vow unsullied by ceremony, sanctified by the look of her eyes into mine and mine into hers. Two people 'in' love, one heart and one soul. It is this and only this no man can put asunder. Weddings be damned.

"Okay," she said. "It's playtime."

6

WHAT NEFFIE MEANT BY PLAY WAS MAKING LOVE, having sex. I had not come across this before. It was not the loose "anything goes" element that was play, and it wasn't the spontaneous "let's do it now, here." It was the guiltless, recreational part, the transformation of sex from its mystical, enshrouded platform into everyday living, a normalcy so easy and natural as to be compared to having a meal or taking a walk, or playing.

This contrasted greatly with my notion of it. I had been taught to approach sex with consecration, with the idea sex was only to consummate an emotional union, to possibly procreate, and was to be treated with deep seriousness. It never occurred to me there was an even more advanced and liberating understanding of this powerful impulse.

I was to find out Neffie's ideas about sex were ideas developed in her as a child, before puberty, and in her training throughout her early years of sexual awakening. She was provided a forum and opportunity to explore her own sexuality and to establish a set of standards and morals to give her the most wonderful and carefree possible sense of herself, and now me.

Because of the narrowness of the canyon, the sun cast the buildings of Welach into shadow early in the afternoon, around three o'clock, and the ground became cool. The day continued full above, the light reflected from the eastern wall back into the city, the result a long twilight with azure skies. When the sun finally set, the angle of reflection became steeper and steeper, causing the colors of the canyon to shine in unimaginable hues as diamondlike daystars began to twinkle through the deeper colors. I lay on the grass in Neffie's arms and fell into a peaceful, dreamless sleep.

When I awoke, it was to the stars above and a distant, almost full moon. Along the edge of the mesa I saw a coyote trotting in the prancing gait given only to animals who live in the wilderness. I wished for him to stop as his silhouette invaded the moon's, to give me the wonderful scene of the coyote sitting on a mesa, head thrown back, howling at the sky while framed by the big yellow circle, but it was not to be. He pranced past the moon into the shadows beyond. Neffie woke up and sat beside me.

"The dance will be starting soon," she said, as she got up and pulled me to my feet.

I had only the tattered clothes I had worn.

"I can find you something to wear," she said, and we climbed the stairs back to her apartment.

Inside, I took some time to look around while Neffie rummaged through her closet and trunks looking for clothes for me. The apartment was bigger than it first appeared, because it went deep into the hillside. There were three more rooms in addition to the front sleeping rooms, and a bathroom with running water and a huge sunken tub carved from the rock, which was also the floor. The back rooms were dark, having no windows, but were lit by lamps. Throughout were some of the most beautiful rugs I had seen, with exquisite patterns and designs, all Native American. Two rooms were sitting rooms of a sort but with no chairs, only pillows and thick rugs, where Neffie and her friends gathered for socializing. The other back room was a kitchen, I think, but I had no way of knowing for sure. It had a small wood-burning stove that might be used for cooking but also may have been for heat. I didn't see any food, but did see a few dishes stored around. Neffie came into the sitting room with some clothes for me to try.

"Where does the electricity come from?" I asked as I pulled the shirt on over my head.

"There is a generator under the creek."

"Under the creek?"

"The creek running down the catwalk has a mirror image underneath it, below ground. We put a generator there and a pump for water."

"Can you drink the water?"

"If you like. It's held in a natural cistern above the city, where it flows in from the bottom and then out over the top into the overground creek, so it's always moving. It's good, clear water. How do those feel?"

I had slipped on the pants she had given me. They fit perfectly, a rough, dark-brown material, heavyweight, almost like canvas but more pliant.

"Great. Whose are these?"

"I don't know," she said as she walked away, into the other room. I knew to ask any more would be impudent; just to shut up and say "thanks."

"They're just right. Thanks."

The shirt was a lighter-colored tan, a soft, blanketlike material with designs familiar to the Southwest: zigzags and diamond shapes in broad lines around the shirt. Neffie came back with a belt and some moccasins. She held out the belt.

It was a series of square conches of beautiful silver laced along a leather strap, which I tied around the outside of the shirt, over the pants underneath. The moccasins were white-soled with dark-red leather tops laced together with strands of rawhide.

"You look wonderful," Neffie said.

I was sure I looked horrible. I had seen many people adopt modern Native American garb and always felt embarrassed for them. Some wounded divorcée, remaking a life with the divorce money, would move to Santa Fe and buy these kinds of garments from the stores around there, usually ribbon-knit God's eyes and feathers on the back of a blue-jean jacket with rhinestone coyotes on the front.

"I hope no one thinks I'm putting on airs," I said.

"They won't if you aren't."

I heard the music. It wasn't what I expected. It was a pounding blues shuffle, and whoever was playing was laying down a groove so deep you couldn't see out of it. The drummer had a foot like a sledgehammer and time like an atomic clock, no easy feat in a shuffle. The bass player was playing simple one-note thumps against the root, the little syncopated skip right before the thud on the beat hanging in the air long enough so you felt yourself sailing from the anticipation to the landing. I never heard a more infectious blues shuffle.

Then the guitar player from hell. Elmore James had this way of sliding to an open D chord by scraping up the guitar neck into a resolution that made me stand up every time I heard it. This player was doing the same thing except with a drive to make me wonder if he didn't have a V-8 somewhere in there, real horsepower, real drag-strip dynamics. This was serious hard-edge blues.

"They're starting. Let's get down there."

As we walked down the outer stairways, we were joined by other people all going the same way. Everyone seemed to know Neffie, she knew everyone, I suppose everyone knew everyone. As we bounced down the stairs and the music grew louder I looked around at the people. Not only was everyone happy—I mean, smiling—they were also beautiful.

I was uncomfortable with this. Happy, smiling, beautiful people on their way to a dance in a magical canyon city beneath the starry moonlit sky of New Mexico, away from the world, in a world of their own. But, there it was. And I was part of it. Of course, I was up to my eyeballs in love, so the glow over everything could have made a root canal seem attractive. The reality is, I don't know what had come into my life, but I will never forget it. Whatever doubt or cynicism that has tried to overtake these memories has failed, and they live on, undiminished and clear.

We got to the bottom and I found we had come to Delilah's again, but things were different. The tables and chairs were gone, so the room was completely open. Earlier there had been a partition across the room, hiding the back, but now I could see it was huge, the size of an amphitheater big enough for five thousand people, a great cave carved into the rock by some ancient wind. There were only about two hundred people, so the room swallowed them. In ordinary circumstances this would look as if the party had failed and needed more people to be festive, but the reverse was true.

Instead, it was as if we had gotten Lincoln Center, or the Rose Bowl, or some airport, all to ourselves and some friends. It was wonderful.

Not as wonderful as the band. Before, I had wished for a camera. Now, I wished for a recorder. But it wouldn't have been any use. It was like a Dead concert. It was of the moment. No recording could have captured it. There were four pieces and a singer-harmonica player.

I have heard horrible, laconic, ugly blues. But when it's right, it's right, and tonight it was right.

The drummer was a thousand-pounder in fringe, with long, straight brown hair below his waist, bright, copper-red skin, and a beak of a nose above an open-mouthed transcendent smile. Every time he hit the drums he sent a shock of air through the cave, blowing through the front door like a shotgun blast. When he played he looked up, not at the drums, holding each stick like a baseball bat.

The bassist was a woman who reminded me of Neffie, tall with long, sandy hair, dressed the same way I had seen Neffie the night she left me with Harouk. But I could pay little attention to her looks, so startling was her bass playing. It was as if in some way she had gotten locked into the foot pedal of the drummer, so every time he hit, she hit. She was playing through a huge stack of amplifiers in back of her, all of it augmented by an enormous stadium-level sound system towering over the band and the stage on each side. They were still playing the shuffle I had heard from Neffie's, and if it was possible, had somehow settled deeper into the pocket.

A part of the vocabulary of drummers is a *flam*, and it basically means two beats played almost on top of each other but a tiny bit out of synch, a kind of *b'dup*. It's usually one of the things wrong when you hear a bad rock band. If one intends to play a flam, fine; it adds interesting color to music, but if you're playing flams because you can't quite play in time with the other players—big trouble. Instead of everyone landing at the same time in the same place . . . *bam*, everyone sort of lands at their own time and in a little different place . . . *kErblytiblAm*. As you might expect, ironing out the flams is hard. That's why the good guys get the big bucks.

Tonight, the closest flam was at Disneyland, a thousand miles away. Every note, every beat was played so perfectly together there was no question the band was of one mind. The guitarist, also a woman, was not as tall as the bassist, her sandy hair in a buzz cut. She was playing slide guitar through another huge set of stacked amps and was also pumping out through the house system.

The keyboard guy was sitting in a circle of some of the greatest instruments ever to play the blues, starting with a black, upright piano he had stashed over to the side of the setup. At the moment he was playing a B3, the big Hammond organ from the sixties, hooked up through a stack of rotating speakers called Leslies. I counted four, two stacks of two, but there may have been more behind him where I couldn't see. He turned on the Leslies in the middle of a riff, and they began to twirl. The sound wailed across the room like thousands of Arabian women calling out across the desert to their returning warrior husbands, billions of wild birds. He hunched over the keys under a black hat with turquoise and beads woven into a hatband. I couldn't see his eyes behind his dark glasses, but his hair was long and sandy, the color of Neffie's.

When the singer came up to the mike the shrill cry of his harmonica sent the energy up another order of magnitude. I don't know what it is about a mouth harp, but the electrified metal reeds reach down inside me and pull up some primitive soul, some basic life force, and shoots sparks off the ends of my fingers. He looked like a banker, a businessman, a clerk. Any of the ordinary people you pass on the street and interact with in an ordinary day. There was no attitude in his short brown hair, or in his jeans and T-shirt. He was wearing round wire glasses and looked like everybody who looks like him. But when he blew the harp you knew this was no average joe, not a typical anybody.

As we all came in and moved around the stage, settling into positions, he let the song loose. He was singing "Get out'the world" a Neftoon Zamora blues tune. I tried as best I could to remember the words. They were something like, "Don't get out'the world 'cause you don't care, just get out'the world cause it's not there."

The life of all Americans comes with a potential arc from Tupelo, Mississippi to Las Vegas, Nevada. We start off cool, then get stranger and stranger. Elvis, of course, is the model for this. He lived this out. Most of the people I know are in some variation of the process of changing from the trim, sexy, leather-wearing Elvis into the fat, beaded, dyed, comb-over Elvis. We may not take the exact path he took but it amounts to the same thing. When we are born into this country we are born with this potential, this Tupelo to Vegas thing, this America gene.

Busting free of such a tendency had always seemed impossible to me, until this night. Something in the air, in the eyes of the people. When they started dancing I knew I had the opportunity to avoid my own personal Las Vegas because somehow each of them had avoided theirs. The dance I had imagined I would see, circular, perhaps around a bonfire with sparks rising into the evening sky, a slow shuffling amid low, droning sounds, was not this dance at all.

This was a dance in front of a band laying down hard blues and soul-motivating shuffles with yet another, more exhilarating difference. This dance was not a mating ritual. There was none of the grinding body parts and sultry looks, no addled, take-me, shake-me, bake-me, your-place-or-the-freeway imperative. This was a dance with people moving to the music because the music took form in the movement, and the people doing the moving were along for the ride, to stand up in the roller-coaster seat and smile and scream, with the music in control.

And could they move. I felt myself getting more and more caught up in this dance, but I was not free enough, didn't understand enough to know what this dance was about. I waved my arms a little but felt silly, embarrassed. It was certain no one was dancing with each other, but everyone was dancing with everyone else. There were no couples. To dance here was to dance more unrestrained and with greater freedom than I ever imagined possible. The more I tried to find the place the dancers around me were sharing, the more self-conscious I became, and the more self-conscious I became, the less conscious I was—of the music, of the time, of the real magic that was no magic, of the heroic pounding of life through hidden veins. At last I gave up and stood there, stupid.

Then I was surrounded, swept up. Neffie beside me and beside her others and all of us together. I think I started doing the mambo. Some Latin thing or other I saw in a movie. Maybe it was the rhumba, but whatever, I was propelled by the power of the music and the joy of those people, catapulted into an orbit so every inhibition, all fear, all self-consciousness left me like gravity leaves a spacecraft as I danced around the room in magnificent abandon and delight.

When the song finally stopped a cheer rose up from us all, including the band. I caught my breath and looked at Neffie.

"I didn't think I could do it."

There was only a second of respite and the music started again, another Zamora tune I recognized from Doc's tape. This time I unhesitatingly threw myself into the fray and careened around the hall on the rails of the music. A fighter pilot pulls less Gs than I did.

Outside all was not calm, and the merriment inside Delilah's was fast being overtaken by a storm. The skies had boiled up and were sweating with rain and New Mexico was about to show some fangs. So much for the placid starlit sky and its sparkling moon. The sky occluded and lowered. Somewhere a monster took aim at the happy band of dancers and their revelry.

When the first snap of lightning flashed it made clear how powerful high-powered blues are, which is to say, not at all. Because right behind the wriggling blue light from the lightning flickering around the dance floor came a clap of thunder so loud it shouted down the hardest hit of the drummer's foot and loudest squeal of the slide guitar.

"You wanna dance?" said nature. "Then dance this."

Another crack of thunder as the rain poured from the sky, a thousand banshees, and the little band of merrymakers slowed, looked outside, and thought about the weather. It sure put a stop to my cavorting.

The little window of the storm I could see out the front door was enough to make me stare. The rain was a solid wall of silver, waving back and forth, obliterating the view.

As the band wound to the end of the tune many of the members of the party walked to the entrance of Delilah's and looked out, debating whether to leave and tuck in for the night.

Then, to their credit, the band, like a dog rolling over on its back in complete subservience, awaiting its master's pat on the tummy, responded by starting into a laid-back, slow blues; well under the power of the storm, acquiescent, introspective; reminding me of ZZ Top's "Rough Boy," but unrecognizable to me. I assumed it was another Zamora tune. The slow pulse meshed with the storm outside and instead of the abandoned twirls around the floor, all the people slowed their pace to the music, and to my surprise, broke off into couples. I looked for Neffie. She was dancing with Artie, RD-Runs Deep. Her head was laid against his shoulder. Talk about stormy blues.

The torrents of my feelings matched the torrents outside. I was struck motionless, and the first needle pricks of the downside of emotional attachment dug themselves into me. I winced. I didn't know what to do. Not only was I a stranger, but my new "wife" had just left with someone else. I felt betrayed and ridiculous. I also felt a hand on my shoulder and was turned around forcefully to face another woman. She said nothing but put herself in my arms and began leading me in a slow dance, forcing me to follow her and the music. I became more disconcerted. I was jealous and feeling foolish. Then to my horror I started to wonder if these people and Neffie were uncommitted and uncommittable. The thought felt like the aftermath of a sucker punch, which hurts more because of the emotion connected with it than the physical pain. I hoped I was wrong but had no way to tell. My unknown partner pulled me close and I felt all of her body against mine.

She was not like Neffie but just as beautiful. All these people had a beautiful concept of themselves. The person dancing with me held me close so I didn't get a long look at her, but I could feel her, see the luster of her sand-colored hair, feel the presence of this beauty, and I knew she was as lovely as Neffie.

After a moment of dancing I eased her away a bit so I could see her face. She had the same perfect features as Neffie but her eyes were an almost coal-black and her skin was a dark-olive tan, almost like an Asian. She had cut her hair to a shoulder length and it curled naturally about her neck. She looked straight at me, with the same familiarity I had come to know from all the people here. Then to my horror I found myself drifting deep into her eyes and falling in love with her. We had not said a word, but the same romantic, loving state of mind overtook me and I wanted to hold this woman and be with her for the rest of my life. I was either hypnotized or going crazy. Who was she? To my further dismay, I felt Neffie vanishing from my affections as easily as they attached themselves to this new person.

I pushed her away as I held on to the edge of panic. Now I could see her clearly. She was gorgeous, like Neffie, with a perfect figure but much smaller, and eyes burning into my soul. I wanted to grab her and kiss her and make love to her right there. She seemed to know this as she came back into my embrace, the casual embrace of the dance, and laid her head on my shoulder and snuggled into it.

I looked around for Neffie but she was gone. I thought I saw her once, but there were so many people here who looked like her, so many with the long sandy hair, and so many of the men who looked like RD, I was unable to pick her out of the crowd. Finally the song came to an end. Whoever she was walked away from me and into the crowd of people at the end of the stage. I started shaking and felt the sweat on my brow. I looked out the door again and saw the rain had slowed to a steady pour, more of a gentle shower. As the band started into another song all I wanted to do was get out of there. I hurried to the front door and stood looking to see if there was a way to get back up to Neffie's under cover. There wasn't, so I walked out into the pouring rain.

The rain was cooling and I welcomed it as it relieved my anxieties and washed the perspiration from me. I was sweating from the fear of my own emotions as well as the rigors of the dance. What had happened to me was new, leaving me without knowing which of my feelings to trust. A few hours before I had been lying on the grass in the canyon floor with Neffie, convinced I had at last found a life partner and then in one mind-snapping turn had seen her dance away with another man while I was swept into the arms of someone for whom the same depth of feeling began anew, the exact same love, for a stranger. I didn't like it at all.

I was drenched in only a few steps and got the wonderful feeling of not caring about getting wet in the rain, so I

slowed and let the rain overtake me, washing me down as
I turned off the walkway along the side of the city to the
canyon floor. I only walked a few feet when I saw
LittleHorse.

He was sitting on a fallen tree and had nothing on except
a thin leather strap around his waist that held a small, beaded
sack on one hip. His body glistened from the water. He was
old, but the way he was built was amazing, with muscles
defined, not a single element of excess. I was startled to see
him, sitting in the rain, deep in thought.

When LittleHorse saw me he nodded a greeting, then
looked up into the rain, past it into the sky, on to something
unseen and unknowable by me, and he lifted his hands up,
palms upward, as if he was feeling the rain, then made a
gesture of turning over his hands with a wave and the rain
stopped. Not instantly, but quickly. The rain came to a
stop at the wave of his hand as surely as if he had turned
it off.

My certainty of the impossibility of the event made its
occurrence stunning. I was taught all my life nothing is impossible, or more precisely all things are possible, but I never
had really allowed the thought the status of fact. My edu-
cation, what I understood of physics, my own sense, told
me only some things can be, so I lived my life within these
confines. All that was instantly rearranged.

"Nice night," LittleHorse said.

Nice night? He was commenting on the weather he had
just changed. I nodded and smiled a weak, "heh-heh" smile.
Little Horse patted the log, motioned for me to sit down as
he slid off of it to sit cross-legged on the wet grass.

"How was the dance?"

When huge motors shut down there is a slow *wrwrrrwrrrrrrwrrrrrrruuuuuhhh*, a sound like an old phonograph record slowing to a stop. Such was the sound I heard now in my own head as most of my belief systems, my bases of navigation and reason, unwound to a halt. I went numb, lost all consciousness of my body and I think I just stared, dumbfounded. Where the hell was I?

There was an expectant look on LittleHorse's face. He was waiting for my answer.

"I got jealous."

"Oh." He nodded. "Then, not so much fun. What happened?"

"Is Neffie your daughter?" I asked.

He nodded. I hesitated. I didn't want to discuss my emotions with him, to have him dissect my jealousies and errant passions, especially about Neffie.

"It is a nice night," I said at last.

LittleHorse looked at me peacefully, sitting in the night, cross-legged, straight, long white hair flowing down his back, green eyes glinting in the moonlight. He was the perfect image of a sage; the wisdom of all times was written across his wrinkled, serene face. I wanted to slug him in the stomach. When he spoke after a moment I was sure he knew my innermost thoughts. I was embarrassed for wanting to punch him. Now I wanted to run away, screaming.

"You might like to try this." He was opening the bag hanging off the leather strap tied around his waist.

Great, I thought. Drugs. Just what I need, some little bit of mushroom or powder so I can see worms crawling in the carpet while I laugh uncontrollably at a knock-knock joke, or drive around a traffic circle for five hours because

I can't get up the courage to merge. Drugs are good for convincing me my mind is utterly subject to the disposition of my body. I hated this idea as much as I doubted it.

LittleHorse held out a pack of peppermint Life Savers.

"I don't like them. Too sweet. What do you think?" He peeled the wrapper back.

I suddenly started to like this guy.

"No, thanks. Too sweet for me too. I'm a salt-and-sour man myself."

"Don't care about food much, taste and stuff. Once I start eating, I can't stop. Appetite runs around, nowhere to go, eat more. RD brought these for me to try but I'm going to give them back." He rolled the Life Savers up and put them back in the bag. I heard a jingle.

"What's in there?" I asked.

He untied the bag and poured the contents out on the ground.

"Car keys, Life Savers, mad money." He pointed to each item he described. The mad money was three quarters.

"You can't get too mad with that," I said.

"I can make a phone call."

LittleHorse looked at me with a huge grin. I didn't know what it meant but it was an innocent, playful smile and I could not help but return it. I did like this guy. I liked him a lot.

"So, who would you call?"

"Nobody. I'm just kidding. Who have I got to get mad at, anyway?"

The moon was framing LittleHorse, creating a rim of blue light around him, the wet grass glistening. Behind him, on a far mesa, I saw another coyote, framed by the moon as well, throw its head back and give the legendary *yip yip yipeeooo*. The guys at Disney sure knew what they were doing, all right. I shivered from the cold.

"I suppose I should go in," I said. "These wet clothes are starting to make me cold."

"Take them off. That's what I do. The evaporation of the water is what's making you cold. Take them off and when you dry you'll be warm."

I stood up and took off everything, then sat on the grass next to LittleHorse. He was right. The clothes were what was cold, so the minute my body dried the warm night air was comforting and felt good. Then, I felt my nakedness.

"Here, put this on and you won't feel so naked." LittleHorse took off the leather strap around his waist and handed it to me.

"Now you'll need this." He held out the empty beaded sack. I took it and nodded my head in thanks. He reached down and dug a pebble out of the dirt beneath the grass and handed it to me. "Put this in there. Magic stone." I laughed.

"No, really." he said. "Throw this magic stone at a magic window and the window will magically break."

I took the stone from him and ceremoniously dropped it into the bag.

"Or secretly put it into the shoe of an enemy and he will magically limp."

I laid back on the grass and looked up at the sky. It was so clear I could see the Milky Way. I'm not much good with constellations but I made out the Little Dipper and the Big Dipper. I have, over the years, made up some constellations of my own, apropos my own self-made astrological chart. Tonight I could see the constellation "Joe, the Terribly Confused." I forgot about Neffie, my jealousy, and the dance. I was happy sitting with LittleHorse. I liked his sense of humor.

"So, LittleHorse, did you stop the rain?"

He nodded.

"How?"

"Practice."

"You know, LittleHorse," I said, "any minute a little dog is going to pull the curtain aside and you're going to say . . ."

"Pay no attention to the man behind the curtain." We both said it together.

"If you like, I will tell you the story of Welach and of our people. I will tell you of Neftoon Zamora and of Chuchen. I will explain my magical powers, but you must promise never to tell another soul."

"I promise," I said.

"Oh, nonsense. Sure you will. I'm just kidding. It's all here for the telling. No, you need keep nothing secret for me. At times, you may want to keep it secret for yourself, but that's a choice you'll have to make on your own. There are times to tell, times to keep quiet. Do you have a camera?"

I shook my head. "No, I wish I did."

"Ah. Should have got one of those little throwaway ones."

"You're right," I said. "But, how did you stop the rain?"

"No, that will come last. You can stop the rain yourself once you have understood what I will tell you. Then I won't need to explain it.

"You must first learn what you can about Welach and

Chuchen. These are cities without time and without history. They are only states of mind, so the history of them and the evolution of them is only ever made up, only ever in the fancies and fantasies of the times. We live in a time of science with a capital *S* and evolution with a capital *E*. So the history of Welach conforms to those notions, much as your own biological history does. And in this scale of time Welach is thousands of years old. We are the oldest continuously inhabited city on earth. Chuchen is our neighbor, but it is nearly impossible to reach for reasons you will discover. It is much like Welach, but with better art and a professional soccer team.''

I sat up.

"Just making sure you were paying attention. A few of us have some of the art from Chuchen. The artisans there have a high understanding of beauty and some here think their art is better than ours. But these art wars are stupid and unimportant. What is important to understand is Chuchen is entirely successful. Here we are still working our way to the place where they have got. Yet, to know more of our world I want you to think a little about your world, the outer world.

"As I am speaking to you everyone in your world is breaking the rules. I mean in the U.S.A., in Europe, all over the world, at some time or another, everyone is in violation of the civil codes. One may not know it, in fact probably does not. But one is either parked in the wrong place, their house isn't up to code, they're behind on their taxes, something. At no time is everyone in full compliance. Right?''

He was. I nodded.

"So the result is you live in a world where everyone is,

in some degree, an outlaw. The reason politicians sound so stupid is because they first try to convince you the rules are right and the people wrong, then they try to convince you more rules will repair the problem. Stupid upon stupid. Especially since the problem is, the rules have become impossible to obey.

''Why is this? How can rules be bad when they have brought so much good? Two reasons. One, there is a confusion of rule and law. You are not living under the law, you are living by rules. And two, unlike law, rules reproduce, evolve, react, and curve back on themselves, becoming like vines allowed to grow over a house. As they get bigger and more entangled, the house itself must finally fall under the weight, and the only thing left is the vine, perhaps dense enough now to provide a little shelter but not like the original house. So what can be done?''

He looked at me, waiting for an answer.

''I don't know. Cut down the vine? Revolution?'' I shrugged.

''Exactly wrong. The vines are the house now. They cannot be cut down. If you pull apart the vines, you work only to the destruction of what little society there is. The only thing to do is to move, to build another house. But people do not do this. They continue to work on the vines, to try to cut them back, retrain them, prune them, graft more vines to them.

''Fortunately you do live in the age of science with a capital S. Even though some science has its own vines growing over the shelter, it is nonetheless a good way to begin. The reason science can help is because it grows in the right way, that is to say, by revelation and insight.

"Look at the moon. It looks as if it revolves around the earth, moving across the sky. In fact, it does. Now look at the sun. It also appears to revolve around the earth as it crosses the sky. How can we tell the sun does not revolve around the earth the way the moon does? Certainly not by looking. They both look the same. Only by revelation and insight can we tell. If you look at the growth of science in the human race you will see most of the great advances have been made by revelation and insight, overturning conventional wisdom, constrained as it is by the physical senses.

"When someone comes along like Newton he moves things along a bit. What happens when Einstein comes along? Does he throw out what Newton has done? No. He presents a larger, more encompassing system of ideas and leaves Newtonian physics where he found it, good for the good it does, but slowly left behind as the larger and better system provides better answers.

"Welach is a city built away from the ordinary world, aware of it, but using it in the ways of Welach, not in the ways of the world.

"We have a document that forms the basis of our social order, like your commandments—quite similar, in fact— but it does not set forth rules of behavior. It states the law, what is so and what is not."

I had to interrupt. "This is a document?"

"I'll give you a copy. The important thing to know is the effect this has on the political economy of Welach. By basing our society on law, the individual is empowered, not restricted. We say, 'you may.' We do not say, 'you may not.' Does that sound like a good idea?"

I nodded.

111

"Would that be a good way to run your world?"

I nodded again.

"Exactly wrong again. Such a notion would create havoc. Your rules of order, which are based on what you may not do, are proper to your times. For one thing it's simpler. 'You can do anything you want . . . except this,' say the rules. That was genius, really inspired, and it worked. Settled everybody right down. Let's say the rule was 'you may only honor one god.' Good rule. Clearly only a rule and not a law, since it certainly seems one may honor as many gods as they want to. Now, what would the 'law' be for something like that? The only thing it could be is 'There is only one god.' That's either true or it isn't. If it's true, then it is a law. If it's a law, it can't be broken. But look at the problem of telling that to most people."

I looked at LittleHorse long and hard. He gave me a slight smile of recognition.

"The wonderful thing about Welach, and the reason you like it here so much, is we are not conforming our behavior to the rules. We recognize the law that governs us, certain it can be no other way. Law by this definition, is truth. With a capital *T*. We live blessedly outside the influences of many of your thinkers. From Rousseau to Freud. From Locke to *I Love Lucy*. We did have a close brush with some Catholics. When we first heard of this teaching, in the 1700s . . .''

"Are you that old?" I asked.

"Of course not."

"How old are you?"

"I don't know. Over a hundred, but I feel great." He did a little hula with his hands. "You want to hear this story or not?"

"Sorry."

"It was when the Spaniards came. They had this story about the head of their religion being a simple, poor man with great powers to heal and control the earth and so forth. We were already doing this a little, so we thought we had found another people like us. When the priest got here, though, it was clear they couldn't heal, couldn't control their world, didn't know who or what did, and they were scaring everybody with this eternal hell thing. Hell you would conveniently fall into if you didn't do what they said.

"When the first really sick and unhappy people asked for help they got a lot of gobbledygook about sinning and being guilty and God being mad at them. So, we knew they were full of rotten lettuce and we came back to Welach and ignored them. It was close, though."

"Do you believe in God?" I asked.

"You tell me what you mean by God and I'll tell you."

"I mean an all . . ."

"No, no. Don't really tell me. That was rhetorical. What I mean is, listen to me, and then you can decide for yourself whether God fits into this or not. It doesn't make any difference whether I believe in God. It only makes a difference whether you do. Let me finish."

"Okay, okay."

"So, the economy of Welach . . . as I say, we had learned how to heal ourselves and to feed ourselves and to live together and work together and play together in harmony. But there was a tension, a desire to grow, to expand, get bigger and bigger. I'm not sure where it came from, but it has only been recently we have found this out and have begun to correct it."

"Correct what? This desire to be a bigger city?"

"No. To propagate in order to maintain the species."

"You think that's wrong?"

"Unlawful."

"Wait, wait, wait." Something in my internal clock had stopped ticking. I didn't like what I was hearing. "You mean die out and not . . ."

"Nez, you are jumping to conclusions and you aren't listening carefully. The idea life is going on because you are having sex, so having children, thereby populating the earth, thereby sustaining life, is just silly. Especially if you understand the universe and our place in it. Learn the history of this city and of the decisions that were made as we went along. Once you have all the facts, you can reconcile this with your upbringing as is best.

"This is a fact. Since we have come to the understanding of certain ideas, Welach has shed itself of its tensions. I can tell because of how good the music is sounding these days. As each day goes by there is a better and better feeling here. When was the last time you sat naked on the ground with an old man and looked at the stars and had pictures come to life? Only Welach provides that."

I sat up and plucked a few pieces of grass from the ground and rolled the leaves into little balls with my fingers. "What kind of work does one have to do to stay here?"

"I'm not sure what you mean," he said. "If you really mean to stay here, very little. If you mean to understand our ways, then you will have to answer your own question with this: If you're walking up a mountain carrying many bags, how much work is it to put down the bags? Understanding the ways of Welach requires patience and listening and watching. You found something of Welach in the songs of Neftoon Zamora. They touched something in you, awakened you to it. This would not have been possible if you had not been listening, would not have been possible with your hands and mind full . . .'' He stopped as he looked up behind me.

I felt a touch on my shoulder and turned, looking up to see Neffie, her long hair blowing around her face, her eyes flashing in the moonlight, focused like a hawk's, lips drawn tight, arms akimbo. She was serious. I stood up quickly and faced her. Something was wrong.

"They found Harouk," she said.

A drop of rain snapped against the end of my nose and rolled off. I looked to the sky, a tufted expanse of darkening gray.

"Where?"

"He was somewhere near the diner. They've gone to get him."

"Is he . . . ?"

"He's alive. They didn't say anything else. I'm going up there. I thought you might want to come."

I did. The little time I had spent with Harouk, I liked him.

"I have to get dressed," I said as I picked up my lump of wet clothes. "Is there something else I can wear?" I offered the clothes as explanation, holding them up for Neffie to see the water oozing from them, dripping between each finger.

"You can check the apartment," she said.

Then LittleHorse looked at me with the same curious

twinkle that had been flashing through his eyes as we talked earlier, but there was a new focus to them.

"The little bag," he said, pointing to the bag he had given me, "is a symbol of male fertility." Another drop of rain landed on my shoulder and ran down my back, right down my spine, giving me a chill, causing me to shudder. "And fertility," he continued, "is best left to the land." He paused. I supposed he was waiting for the remark to register its importance. I didn't have any idea what he was talking about.

"You better get going." He looked up. "It's starting to rain."

I remember having the usual stack of dreams about being naked in a public place, mixed in with the dreams of being unprepared, dreams of having to take a test or perform some piece of music, recite some poetry, and having no idea how to do it. Standing there with LittleHorse and Neffie I felt profoundly naked and unprepared. My moment in the enchanted land of mystical houses was turning into a childhood nightmare. I wanted to cover up. The raindrops were coming more frequently and running along my legs and torso.

I looked toward Delilah's and saw the crowd coming from the door. The dance was over. I held my bundle of wet clothes in front of me, low, covering, and looked to the top of the staircased apartments at Neffie's. It might as well have been the moon. To walk those stairs, with all those people, was an impossibility for me at that moment.

"I'll go get you some clothes," said Neffie. "You can stay here and hide behind this log."

She walked away toward her apartment. LittleHorse uncrossed his legs and stood up without touching the ground

with his hands. He smiled at me like a waiter saying "I'll
be with you in a moment," and walked away, across the
valley floor. He was, of course, completely naked, since I
now had his little bag and the leather thong that held it
around my waist.

I was alone. I felt humiliated and foolish. I looked at the
ball of wet clothes in my hand and began to unfold them.
The rain came now in a gentle shower and I put on the
sopping pants and shirt as I looked at the log Neffie said I
could hide behind.

The walkways were emptying as everyone in the town
of Welach went to their apartments. No one looked at me
or LittleHorse, no one strayed from the walkways. Soon the
town looked asleep.

I was soaked. As the new rain began to pour there were
currents of water along my body. I sat on the log and tried
to put on the moccasins, but they were soggy and wouldn't
slide over my foot. I gave up after a few tries and decided
to go to Delilah's, the nearest shelter. As I walked I looked
toward Neffie's apartment. There was no sign of her.

Inside Delilah's it was warm and dry and empty except
for a sole figure near the stage who was packing up the last
of the band gear. He turned as I came in, looked at me for
an instant, then resumed his work. A single white light
bulb from the top of a portable stand was the only source
of light. It rang out into the huge cavern in a sphere of
diminishing visibility, carving hard shadows behind all it
touched.

I sat in one of the chairs and tried to get the moccasins
on again but still had the same trouble. I let them drop to
the stone floor and watched the man finish packing the last

bit of equipment, close up the box he had opened, and leave by a side entrance.

Once again I was alone. This time it was eerie; the light in the cave from the little bulb was not enough for me to see anything immediately around me, and outside the rain began to escalate in volume, in water and sound. The entrance to Delilah's closed over again with the silver sheet I had seen at the dance.

I walked to the doorway and looked out at the city, a dim outline through the torrents. I could not have seen Neffie if she had been coming. Then something happened to me I cannot explain.

It was another wave of emotion but it was not the presence of a feeling. It was the absence of all feeling. No sensibility of any kind. I stood looking at the rain for a few seconds, then, in a lifeless shuffle, walked back to the chair I had been sitting on and carefully lowered myself down. All thoughts were leaving me, all thoughts about thoughts were leaving me.

I did not care about anything. The feeling was neither good nor bad, it was no feeling, a type of emotional numbness, the disappearance of my mind. Not of my consciousness, but of all the ideas that usually rolled around in my thinking. This was accompanied by a state of desirelessness, of having no goal, nowhere to be, wanting nothing, nothing to investigate or discover.

From a distance I heard music. I didn't know if it was from inside my head or outside. It seemed like the music I heard when I was with Neffie in her apartment, when the band had first started to play, but it was not as clear and it was not the blues. It was an unknown type of sound, mu-

118

sical, but without any of the usual musical clues. It filled my thinking completely, rushing up like water filling a bowl, shutting out all else.

There are case studies of people whose thinking was arrested in some trauma, who never aged, who never moved beyond the moment of their arrest. These people all displayed remarkable physical properties. A seventy-year-old woman had the body of a nineteen-year-old, the age she was when her lover was killed. Of course, she was mad, because she did not have the mind of a nineteen-year-old and she did not have the mind of a seventy-year-old. She was caught in a loop, circling back upon itself, never leaving the instant of her emotional trauma, never really living the life that passed in front of her for the next fifty-one years.

This music in my head had that same horrible quality of agelessness without growth, of a static perfection defying time. It increased in volume until it became as a mighty and rushing river, all the sounds melting together in a roar. The sonic spectrum surpassed everything I had ever heard with my ears, low tones deeper than the center of the earth, high tones like the cracking of teeth and bones. All the ages were in this sound, and there was no essence of music anymore, only a complete and overpowering constant hum, a power hum, like a stuck electric motor.

Outside the rain had stopped but I did not notice. Neffie was in the doorway, a gray silhouette, holding some dry clothes.

As she walked to me I saw in her eyes a flicker of recognition. She knew what I was going through. I stared at her blankly. I did not feel the warmth of love rise in me as

I had before. I felt no connection to her at all. I did not feel jealous of RD or competitive.

Neffie was simply another figure on a strange landscape of some type of dementia. As she came close to me, face-to-face, the noise in my head began to subside, the sounds diminishing in a way that was not like the volume decreasing, but like the dissipation of a mass, the dispersal throughout my being of particles of sound.

Neffie stroked my brow and smoothed my hair back. She wiped the water from my face and began to pull the sodden shirt off my shoulders. She took every piece of clothing from me and wiped the water off me with her hands. The clothes she had brought with her were my old clothes, the ones I had been wearing when I had come here, but they were clean, freshly washed, and the tears from the fall were sewn and repaired.

I began to dress myself with her help. I took the leather pouch from around my waist and pushed it into the pocket of my blue jeans. When I was fully dressed Neffie embraced me, holding me in her arms tightly for a long while.

"Now, listen to me." She grabbed me by my shoulders and forced her gaze into mine. "In the transition you call death you will see the same thing again you are seeing now. The music will turn into light and the light will turn into you. But, there is nothing in this. Nothing to be made of it. No one dies. We have to get Harouk. That is the next stage of the story here. So come with me. Here. LittleHorse said you wanted this."

She held out a coin. It was the size of a U.S. silver dollar. I looked at it and saw it was covered with markings; not a writing I recognized as foreign, but marks I could not decipher. I held it in my hand. It was light, something like aluminum, not quite round, and flimsy. I held it for a second before closing my fingers around it.

I pushed it into the watch pocket of my jeans. I felt my mind restarting, an onset of grossness as I contemplated the tasks at hand, a feeling of sinking back to earth after having floated weightless.

Neffie took my hand and led me from Delilah's. The clouds still blocked the sky but the rain had stopped. Outside we turned away from Welach, down a stone-paved path leading along the side of the canyon. I followed Neffie along the walk and knew I would never see this city again. I looked back to take a picture in my mind and saw the magnificent dwellings stacked one on the other carved from the side of the hill, a great monument, at once a part of the land and yet built as only the might of intelligence can build. An intelligence beyond the intelligence of mortals. The city glistened from the fresh rain and then slid into the fog that had settled along the canyon floor.

The path led into a tunnel carved from the hillside. Inside the tunnel were shallow steps leading down for a long distance. We walked in the tunnel for perhaps fifteen minutes until we emerged into a clearing much lower than where we started. Here I could see the stars.

The clearing was big, stretching across a wide valley, surrounded on all sides by low hills and mesas. We walked along a footpath for almost a mile until we came to a break in the surrounding hills, a little canyon. Then through this we were at a grove of ponderosa, surrounding an open, flat space where Neffie's motorcycle and three cars were parked:

121

mine, a Honda Prelude, and a perfect 1972 El Camino SS. It was bright yellow.

RD was standing by the car with two other men, both as big as he. As Neffie and I walked to the car I felt a twinge of the old jealousy, but it quickly passed. That was the last time I felt it. Then from the bed of the El Camino came a low moan as Harouk raised himself up into a sitting position.

"Are you all right?" Neffie asked.

"No, I'm not all right," Harouk said. "I think I broke every bone in my body."

"Did you get shot?"

Harouk raised up further in the back of the bed and pulled himself to the side. He uncoiled, crawled over the bedsides and stood up outside the little truck, then stretched like he was waking up from a long sleep.

"No. That guy couldn't hit anything with a gun. I'm okay, really, just banged up. You obviously got away."

Neffie nodded yes. "I slipped out the side door and came in the back way to Welach. Nez was in Glenwood and followed me in."

This impressed Harouk.

"The back way?" he said, pointing the remark, but it was lost on me.

Harouk walked around, stretching his arms some more. Neffie walked to RD, gave him a hug and waved thanks as he and the other two men climbed into the Prelude and drove off, leaving the three of us alone.

Harouk let the tailgate down on the bed of the truck and hopped up to sit on it. Neffie sat beside him.

"What happened?" Neffie asked.

"I ran across the road when Gus started shooting and

laid down in the acequia. When he backed out, to chase you, he ran over my foot. The acequia was muddy, so it pushed my foot down into the muck. Didn't hurt, but it stuck me there. Then, when every emergency vehicle in the world started to show up at the diner, one of the ambulances backed into the ditch and ran over me.''

"You got run over by the ambulance?'' I said, incredulous and trying not to laugh.

Harouk did laugh. "*An* ambulance. Four came.''

"I'm glad it strikes you funny too,'' I said.

"It didn't at the time. It could have been terrible. But because the bottom of the acequia was so mushy I kept getting pushed further and further into the clay. I didn't want to scream because I didn't want to be involved in the whole scene. I think Li called the cops or whatever.''

"Did he get hit?'' Neffie asked.

"I don't know. I don't think so. He went down behind the counter so I couldn't see. I just wanted to get out of there. There were cops and paramedics for days. Since it was after-hours everybody around there with an ambulance responded, looking for the overtime. I counted four ambulances and twelve cop cars.''

"Twelve?'' Neffie said.

"Yep. Of course there wasn't one fire truck and when the diner caught fire . . .''

"You're kidding,'' she said.

"No, really. Caught fire, from Li maybe, on purpose or not, but up she went. There were twenty uniforms standing around watching the place turn to toast. No fire truck for thirty minutes . . . came just in time to hose down the ashes.''

"And you were in the ditch all this time?" I asked.

"Yeah, the ambulance that rolled over me, rolled right off so I laid there. I wasn't hurt and I could breathe. . . ."

"But didn't you say you broke every bone in your body?"

"Not literally. I was talking about the ride up here, Nez. I was in the back of this truck. The last five miles over this rocky road was a nightmare."

"So the diner's gone?" Neffie said.

"All gone," said Harouk. "I wish you could have been there, though. The best part was . . . I'm stuck in the clay, the diner burns down, all the officials are standing around . . . some of them had little car–fire extinguishers and tried to use them, which was as silly as it looked . . . and then, when the place is finally a pile of cinders, the fire truck comes . . . pumps enough water to make a plume of smoke the size of the Rose Bowl . . . decide to try to pull myself out of there and split. I worked for a few minutes, got loose, and . . . stood up. Man, you shoulda seen it. In all this white smoke and red-and-blue flashing lights, this guy stands up from the ditch totally covered with gray and red clay. . . . I mean, the place went nuts. They started yelling, all sure they were seeing, like, the 'fire ghost' or some monster. If I had had my wits about me I could have scared them out of some money or something. I mean, they were petrified with fear. Instead I got the hell out of there. It was a pretty good time, though."

"And Li?" Neffie asked.

"Never saw him. Not for sure. I guess he must have been talking to the cops, but I never saw him. I went to the hunting cabin back up by our place and hid out there. I guess RD sent his guys out—they're the ones that found me.''

''I told him to look for you,'' said Neffie. ''I was worried. I didn't know whether you had been hit or not.''

''Thanks. No, not a scratch. I'm fine. Did you ever find Kweethu?''

''What do you mean?'' Neffie said, concerned.

''You know she was in the car with me and Gus?''

''No.''

''Yeah. Absolutely. Gus picked her up in Quemado. Made her come with him to the diner. She was in the backseat. Didn't you see her?''

''No,'' she said again. This time her concern was up a notch, but it seemed to me an odd concern, not just about Kweethu's safety, but more as if Neffie had been given a call to action she had missed.

''When Gus took off out of there, after you, she was with him. Have you checked to see where she is?''

Now Neffie was clearly focused. She sensed something of extreme importance to her. I thought it might be the shock of Kweethu being kidnapped mixed with some sense of a greater danger. Those emotions were present, I think, but there was more to it than that, much more, hidden to me.

''It never occurred to me. I thought you were alone in the car. We better go up to Quemado and check. You feel up to a drive?''

This last remark was to me.

''Sure.''

We all climbed into the front seat of the El Camino and

drove down the bumpy road to the highway and, I think, turned toward Quemado. I say "I think" because there were no road signs at the junction. I watched everything as closely as I could with one objective: to find my way back to We- lach. But I couldn't pinpoint any landmarks or signs. There was no moon now and my private constellations were use- less. Knowing "Clementine the Rude" is a good way to amuse myself, but no way to navigate.

When we pulled onto the paved road it was a relief from the grinding bumps of the previous four and three-tenths miles. I did have the good sense to look at the odometer.

Neffie was driving and I was sitting between her and Har- ouk. My legs were up underneath me, on the transmission hump. The light from the dash lit Neffie's face; the road un- wound before us into the New Mexico countryside. We were silent, nothing to say or do but watch the road unfurl. My thoughts drifted over the events of the last days and I flexed my wrists and fingers, still amazed at the quick recovery.

As we drove through the night, and the road began to twist around the hills, I felt Welach drift away. Perhaps I would come and look for the city again. But, perhaps not. The road before me overtook my attention gradually, until it was all I was thinking about.

Over the distant mesas the sun began to cast its first light. I had stayed up all night again. My biological clock had been confused since I left Doc's.

I MET DOC when I was in high school. He came to the school to give one of those talks on hygiene and there was something about him that drew me to him. After his lecture

I approached him and we started a conversation about hot rods. I was a car nut in high school and was thrilled to find a semi-adult—he was in his twenties—who knew anything about cars or was willing to talk about them.

He seemed knowledgeable about some of the more arcane aspects of car building and customizing, but he was most familiar with the elements of the car, with the concept of a car, as a system of ideas. He was the first to point out to me nothing man-made existed that didn't first exist as an idea. This was the first glimpse I had into the power of ideas.

He also was the first to point out to me a fundamental flaw in the structure of American society, namely that the hierarchy of our society was based on needless skills, creating a society whose value system was at odds with its own historical realities and the realities of the world.

Doc's notion was the greatest men and women of history have a clear order of importance relative to their effect on our lives.

At the top of that order are the spiritual leaders who can and do alter our perception of reality. Behind them, a close second, are the thinkers, philosophers and poets, writers and artists and scientists.

Beneath them by a significant degree are state leaders and governors of some type: kings, presidents, emperors, and lawmakers.

Next are the adventurers, including businesspeople of great wealth and philanthropy, and inventors, the appliers of science and technology.

Where on this list, he asked me, are the great athletes? How far back does our memory go of people with extraordinary physical skills? A hundred years? Barely. Do you

remember the sport of archery diving? Jumping off a diving
board into a swimming pool while shooting a bow and
arrow at a target? Of course not.

But look at the structure of high school society, that
little model of American society, and you see a pecking
order that is the complete reverse of the historical order
of importance. Athletes are the most popular, the most
valuable (because of the income they generate), the most
socially important. The best male athletes get the prettiest
girls and the best female athletes get whatever they want.

Next are the wealthy, the locally powerful, especially
if they are physically beautiful. And way down on the list,
derided and abused, lowest on the high school popularity
index, are the poets, philosophers, artists, scientists, and,
very last, the spiritual thinkers, usually considered crack-
pots. When we leave high school it takes ages to shake off
this social order. Some never do, dying drunk on beer in
front of the latest sporting event, looking for a hero, a role
model, where none exists.

I liked the way his thinking developed along these lines.
I also knew the ideas were dangerous, the kind likely to
get you killed a few centuries ago and get you mutilated
today or at least ostracized. Try going into a sports bar on
Super Bowl Sunday, turning off the TV and reciting a
poem, and you'll see what I mean.

I looked in the rearview mirror of the El Camino and
could see my scraped-up face, behind me the road wandering into the early-morning horizon. On the horizon
stood Rousseau. I remembered his dismal admonitions to
avoid artists and menstruating women, since one was useless and the other was, well, useless too. His figure loomed

smaller and smaller until the sunrise, in one exploding ray over the purple mesa, turned him into a silhouette wavering like a flame, then extinguished.

We turned off the paved highway and drove along a smooth dirt road for a mile or so until we came to an enclave of five or six small adobes arranged in a great circle.

Breakfast was under way, tiny wisps of smoke from the chimneys on the little houses wafted into the pink morning sky, carrying the smell of tortillas and fried beans. A black dog walked up to the car as we came to a stop outside the circle and looked in as Harouk and I got out of the passenger side. When the dog saw Neffie he became excited and ran to her, spinning in circles and jumping with glee, rising on his hind legs to lick her face.

Neffie ruffled his fur and caressed him. Two young children playing in front of the houses saw Neffie and had nearly the same reaction as the dog, running to her in abandoned delight, jumping into her arms and smothering her with kisses.

Neffie picked the youngest one up and walked toward the biggest adobe. The excitement of the children stirred the people in the houses and more and more of them came outside.

Soon Neffie was surrounded by fifteen or so people, all Native American, from small children to adults, thrilled to see her. One of the smaller children crawled into her other arm so now she had a child on each one. Neffie made her way to a bench carved from a solid piece of wood and sat down.

Everyone wanted to touch her. The children climbed on her seated figure until she was virtually covered, a child on each leg, one standing on each side of her, four at her

129

feet and adults standing about her, waiting. I had never seen such love expressed for someone as these people expressed for Neffie.

I looked at Harouk, but he did not return my gaze. Instead, he was looking at the scene before us, smiling, familiar with such a response for Neffie, knowing it would happen and happy to see it had.

From a small adobe came an old woman who I thought was Kweethu. But as she came closer I could see she was not the same person I had met in the parking lot in Quemado. I was to learn this was her sister. Neffie beckoned to her and the woman came to Neffie. The children parted enough to give her room, respectfully, but not enough to let go of Neffie completely, holding to her like treasure.

"Have you seen Kweethu?" Neffie asked.

The woman shook her head but did not speak.

One of the children said, "She's playing bingo."

The child next to him elbowed him in the ribs and said, "No, she isn't. You're stupid."

"I saw her in town," a little one said.

To all of these sightings, the old woman shook her head to Neffie's questioning glances.

"How long?' Neffie asked the old woman.

The woman said something in a language I didn't understand. I looked again at Harouk, but he still looked only at Neffie. She stared at him for a second and he nodded some understanding. Neffie shuffled in her seat and the children closed in on her again. Kweethu's sister sat on the bench next to her.

"Do you have a story to tell us?" one of the older girls asked.

This sent the other children into cries of ecstasy, pleading with Neffie to tell a story.

Neffie looked on these people gathered about her with more love than I am able to describe. Something went out from her eyes and her heart to them, something tangible and alive, something like compassion, but more a mixture of care and camaraderie, at once their equal as children, then as their teacher.

"Okay," she said. "A short one." She looked at me and Harouk.

"That man over there is Nez." She pointed to me with her eyes. Everyone turned and looked at me. I wanted to faint, run, hide. I looked behind me for someplace to go. It was that moment when the magician picks you from the audience to come up to the stage to help him with a trick and you know he is going to pour water on you or tear up your clothes or smash your watch. I gulped and produced this idiotic good-natured smile. Then I sort of shook my head. To this day I have no idea what I was saying "no" to.

"Nez is a wise man and knows a lot about frogs."

Frogs?

"There is a story the people of Chuchen tell of the frog man. A frog was out plowing a field one day and an angel appeared and said, 'you have been chosen to build a great temple for the king. Will you come with me in my golden chariot?' Well, the frog was tired from working in the field all day and said no. The angel left and never came back. When the frog got home that night he told his wife, the loon, what had happened and she became crazy with jealousy. 'You let an angel from the king get away?' she

screamed. 'Why, that would have been food for a month.'
This legend has kept the people of Chuchen entertained for
years, even though there is not a shred of truth to it. Until
today. Now that Nez has come looking for Kweethu with
me that story of the frog and the field and the loon for a
wife has even less meaning, just the crazy ramblings of a
lost culture. So, now, Nez. Tell us what you love,'' Neffie
said.

What did I love? Well, let me think.

"I love you, Neffie."

Everyone nodded approval at this. I was not alone in
this notion, it was obvious. However, this was not the
answer.

"And I love warm winds."

This caused a ripple in the crowd, a damn of faint
praise. The children knew it was a weak answer; too New
Agey.

"I love to laugh." I rose the inflection on the end of
the statement, but left out any question.

That was the hot button, the magic trick. I got a round
of applause as the children stood up, their faces alive with
delight, and cheered. Neffie stood at the same time. She
walked to me and embraced me and laughed. She put one
arm around my waist. "Welcome," she said as she swept
her other hand across the scene, presenting me, "to
Chuchen."

At that instant I fell into a quiet, indescribable peace. I
was through the looking glass, with the White Rabbit and
the Mad Hatter and Alice. I was elated and confused, happy
and perplexed.

I turned to look at the El Camino, shining yellow in

the morning, a golden chariot if there ever was one. I was swept up in the arms of these people, absurdly, without a narrative, living in a moment of eternal happiness. From here I could see forever, the road trip ahead of me, the people I would meet, the dangers that would come and go, and through it all, the children wrapped around the feet and arms of Neftoon Zamora, laughing as the fish ate my furniture. I have never had much tolerance for 'gee whiz' in my life, but now, standing at this miraculous spot, waiting for the next part of the story to unfold, it was the only thing that came to mind.

7

WAS THIS LITTLE GROUP OF ADOBE HUTS CHUCHEN, the magical city? The only figure that matched my expectations of the trip so far was Neffie, her tall and lean bearing as she towered above the people around her making her appear a mythical figure. Her sandy hair, so distinct from the shiny coal-black hair of the locals, set her further apart, a gem in its setting.

For one second, I saw a light, the tiniest glimmer of insight. While I was looking for a stable pattern of events, Neffie was showing me perturbations, wrinkles. The laughter of Chuchen was not an anomaly in some narrative perfection, it was only what needed to be different enough for the city to evolve, to move to the next step. The magic of the music on the tape suddenly was with me here, the same precious moment, repeated in the eyes of the Chuchinas, and it was causing a subtle shift, a change; this unusual and powerful instant was changing everything. Then, like a falling leaf, I rocked slowly back and forth, gently, to the earth. Neffie pulled me back to the next stage of the journey.

"Tonathu says Kweethu has been gone for over a week," Neffie said to both of us, but more to Harouk than me.

The children and villagers returned to their normal routines. One young boy—about ten—brought out a plate of tortillas and beans from one of the houses and offered it to me. I was starving. I hadn't realized the foul food of Welach had left me so hungry. I happily accepted the plate and put it down on the roof of the El Camino, hoping this food would be at least edible. It was. I ate every bite. Harouk and Neffie weren't the least interested in the food. I knew this about Neffie. I was learning it about Harouk.

"I think we should go to the center," said Harouk.

Neffie knew what this meant.

"Should we drive or teleport?" she asked.

I looked at her, startled.

"Only kidding," she said to me. Then, to Harouk, "How long do you think it would take? Do you know where it is?"

"I have a general idea," he said. "Li told me it was in southeastern Arizona. I think there was an address on his pamphlets . . . or we could call."

Out of his shirt pocket Harouk pulled his phone, covered with mud, flipped it open and dialed. The phone didn't work.

"Then again, maybe not."

"It can't be more than a few hours. We'll get in the area, then ask. Are you up for this?" Neffie said to me.

I was beat, worn down from the pace and content of the last few days. I desperately needed to sleep.

"I'm fine. Yeah. Great," I said.

"Why don't you lay down in the back? I'll borrow a pad," Harouk said as he opened the tailgate of the El Camino and brushed out the little bit of dust gathered there. He walked to one of the houses and came back in seconds with a sleeping bag, which he unrolled. I was happy at the prospect of sleeping for a few minutes, at least.

I climbed in the truck bed, lay down, and fell fast asleep as Neffie and Harouk drove out of the little circle of houses.

When I awoke it was late afternoon, the sun was hot, beaming down. We had stopped in a service station.

Service stations along the more remote stretches of road can occupy hundreds of acres, which makes for some amazing service stations. We had stopped at one of the more remarkable ones. It stretched over acres and acres of asphalt, on which were parked hundreds of long-haul trucks. In back of the station was an oil refinery. I don't think there was an oil well there, only the refinery, which bought the crude oil, refined it on the spot, and pumped it to the station— fresh gas.

The station itself was thousands of square feet in the front building. The rest of it looked like a city, and the whole thing was isolated, solitary; no other building as far as one could see in any direction, only this huge service station built in recluse over the Arizona desert floor and nothing else around. Nothing.

Unless, of course, you count the saguaro cacti standing sentry, the sage and mesquite, *chamisa* and ponderosa, the shining sand glittering with mica and onyx, crystal and shale, the cuneiform mountains describing the horizon, and the sky a blue so beautiful it made you blink. The gargantuan GAS sign, glowering down from its perch, dared me to think of all that as "something."

I crawled out of the bed of the truck and stretched as Neffie and Harouk came from the cab. Harouk was ebullient.

"I love this," he said. "I'll go pay for the gas."

He almost skipped to the main building.

"I think he likes this place. Have you been here before?"

I asked Neffie as she began pumping gas into the car. She shook her head no.

"He likes the mind-boggling aspect; something like this out here." She swept her hand along the horizon, the wide-open spaces. "Watch, he'll come back with a souvenir."

"I think I'll go inside as well," I said.

Neffie nodded and we agreed to meet in a few minutes in the main hallway.

When I got inside I understood more about Harouk's excitement, though I did not share it. The place was like the inside of a mother ship, a place that was creating the world in itself, not subject to the outside in any way.

The main hallway was the size of a highway, approximately seventy-five feet across, and down each side were storefronts in a cacophony of colored sales banners, all offering travel-related goods. The people were itinerant, mostly truck drivers, dressed casually for the road and maintaining an attitude of living on their own, a transient sensibility. This was no hometown mall. A clothing store had racks of blue jeans and boots, baseball hats with bizarre phrases printed across the front of them, bags of fifty socks or fifty underwear at prices low enough to wear once and throw away, avoiding the dreaded Laundromat. Nowhere was there formal wear or anything for dressing up, no jackets or ties or evening gowns. The store was only for the utilitarian clothing of the road.

Other stores were just as specialized, and huge. A tool store, selling only hand tools and things for roadside repairs. A radio shop selling expensive CB radios. A music store selling only country-and-western music. A grocery store selling snack foods easily eaten by hand from the lap. A toy store selling gifts to take home to the children. It was called "Molly's." Short, I figured, for *mollify*.

The hallways were loaded with people. If it was possible, these hallways the size of the interstate felt crowded. Most of the patrons had gathered around three fast-food restaurants: a Taco Bell, Burger King, and Grandma's Kountry Kitchen.

I walked toward Grandma's with the idea I would get something to eat before we got back on the road. I could not account for my sudden intense attention to diet and rest. Maybe it was because Neffie and Harouk were apparently without appetite, yet possessed with endless energy, and I was more and more concerned I might find myself embarking on a three-day hike having failed to eat or sleep for the previous three days.

Like everything else in this search for the blues, Grandma's was twisted. The two *K*'s in the name were a hint. I should have taken it.

I parked myself in line and could see the buffet clearly from where I was standing. The steam table was, oh, roughly one square mile. Over near one end was a general aviation airport where cargo planes loaded with food for the starving in "insert name of starving country here" were taking off and landing. Tiny people, crushed by the perspective of distance, would start at one side of the buffet table and work their way around, piling on metric ton after ton of biscuits and gravy and sausage and bacon and eggs and hash-brown potatoes and driving forklifts and steam cranes to pick up the . . . no, I won't do this to you. Trust me. The place was big.

Beyond this "all-day breakfast bar," the restaurant itself

lay like a cathedral, supposedly to inspire—actually to intimidate—to get your money and get you out, to "turn" the
table and make room for the next person. At first it would
look inviting, then one would become more uncomfortable
with each moment, until finally, inundated with the noise,
visual and aural, one had to get out of there.

The plastic booths and spill-camouflaged carpet looked
as rugged and indestructible as the bathrooms, and as easily
cleanable. Somewhere there must have existed a machine
that showed up between three and four in the morning, and
in one great blast of disinfectant and cleaning fluid returned
the place to its native condition of sparkling cleanliness, erad-
icating all traces of the humanity that had come through
there, and leaving behind only a faint trace of pine scent.
Not the place to fall asleep, or read a book, or get lost.

I had always thought astronomers were the only ones
that dealt with size like this, using numbers so great words
had to be invented to describe their scale and measure,
words like *light-year* and *parsec*. But I could see the really big
numbers were in modern food service. It is as impossible
for me to understand the distance to our nearest star as it
is for me to understand the number of tomatoes a national
burger chain sells in an hour.

My turn finally came to get my ticket and go to the
buffet, but I had lost my appetite. I thanked the lady, who
seemed upset by the fact I was willing to throw away all
my time in line, and walked into the main hallway, shrinking
a little.

I walked slowly along looking at the storefronts, past the
video-game parlor with its *gweeps* and *warps* and *dwipples*, past

the espresso bar next to the hot-dog stand, the smells intermixing, mustard, popcorn, coffee, licorice. The young woman behind the counter of smells had bottom-feeder hair: hair meticulously arranged so tiny wisps shot out over her face in curious little dangling curls, reminding me of pictures I had seen of fish supposed to live on the ocean floor where no sun shines, having developed similar appendages that hang tiny, bioluminescent lanterns over their eyes and mouth so they can see.

The floors were as shiny as a still lake. The glass windows and doors smudge-free, crystalline. I was walking farther and farther into the heart of a mother ship swept completely clean, polished down to its perfect synthetic surface, a permanent, indestructible surface, waiting for generation after generation of cleaners to come and service it, when it hit me. Service it. The *service* station. The place where we humans served. Who was serving who . . . or what? I had this strong and clear feeling I should turn around and get outside as quickly as possible. From inside this beast, the only clue I had I was on Earth was gravity. Everything else was artificial, except for the humans sucked in from the road. Next to me a young man asked an apparent stranger if he knew where he could get an employment application. I hurried on, flowing with the peripatetic crowd.

The piazzas of Italy and the buildings of hundreds of years ago were built to pedestrian scale. When America industrialized it created a new scale: automotive scale. But this service-station mall superdrome was another scale entirely. Not pedestrian, not automotive, more the scale of imagined need.

Harouk came up behind me and tapped me on the shoulder. He held out a prepackaged fried apple pie, snack-sized, and a cold bottle of prebrewed tea.

"I got these for you, in case you were hungry. I want to check in here. I'll be right back."

I sat on one of the benches in the great hallway and marveled for a moment at Harouk's sensitivity. He went into Grandma's Kountry Kitchen, past the line and to the back of the restaurant, out of sight. Neffie was walking up the hallway toward me and sat down on the bench as Harouk reappeared.

"Good," she said. "You got something to eat."

That was good news too. I suppose I didn't need to worry about Harouk and Neffie enlisting me in their level of non-eating. After all, it had been Neffie who had fed me in Welach, even though the food was awful. Comforted thus, I set the food aside, next to a trash can built so well it could have been used for shelter in case of nuclear attack.

"They had dozens. The address is on the bottom but it's a p.o. box." Harouk was holding an Augie Rootliff pamphlet, *Just How Far Is It?*, showing it to Neffie as he pointed out the address of the Rootliff Center on the bottom of the back page.

As she looked at it, Harouk looked away, when suddenly all the muscles in his face tightened and his eyes widened. I glanced in the direction of his look, then back to him. He pulled the pamphlet from Neffie and turned his back to us.

"Neffie. By the tool store, just going in."

She looked in the same direction as Harouk had, then she too, quickly turned her back to me.

In front of the tool store, standing over a bin of one-dollar tools, looking at a cheap hammer, was a man who resembled a slightly overweight, balding movie star.

"Nez," said Neffie. "Watch where that man goes. It's Rootliff."

"Rootliff?"

"Gus. The man with the gun at the diner. He's Augie Rootliff. Watch him. We're going in here. We can see you. Follow him when he leaves; we'll follow you."

What do I mean by movie star? Someone a movie camera and a big screen can enhance enough to contain our own projections of ideals. The man fingering the hammer was ordinary in the extreme except for the cut of his jaw, the shape of his eyes, features that live in the two dimensions of a mirror or a camera better than they live in the world. His tan skin and brown eyes were contrasted by white slacks and, worn outside the pants, a white casual shirt with four pockets on the front. The outfit was finished off with a giant turquoise stone in a bolo tie, silver and turquoise bracelets, and a pair of light-brown Clarke desert boots. He put the hammer down and walked into the tool store. I got up and moved to a spot across the hallway where I could see him.

He shopped around the store for a few minutes, then he shoplifted a small tape measure; stuffed it in his pocket, and walked out. I almost burst out laughing. Fortunately I held the laughter in, for at that moment Augie came out, nonchalant; he may have even whistled, shoving his hands in his pocket and beginning a stroll along the interior interstate, window-shopping, a petty thief.

I didn't have any idea what to do. I was supposed to follow him, but I knew at some point he would notice me. I had no idea how to go about clandestine activities, how to follow someone without getting noticed, or eavesdrop, or window peep. I took up a position a few feet behind him and walked along at his pace. He looked at me several times and I smiled, kind of a "I'm not really here" smile. But finally I felt so silly and obvious, I had to walk past him, out the front doors, and over to the El Camino.

Seconds later he came out of the service station and seconds after that so did Neffie and Harouk.

For whatever reason he took no further notice of me, or Neffie and Harouk. Instead he walked to a new Cadillac, got in and drove away.

"Now what?" I asked.

"We follow him," said Harouk, opening the door for me to slide in the middle, between him and Neffie, who was driving.

"You'll have to excuse me for being stupid," I said as I got in the car, "but are we really going to follow him down a deserted stretch of Arizona highway in a bright-yellow El Camino and not get noticed?"

"Sure," said Neffie. "He'll never see us. He's nothing if not completely involved with himself."

I didn't know Augie, or Gus, or whatever his name was, so I had no notion of whether that was true about him, but it was definitely something I had noticed about Cadillac drivers. As Augie's shiny white Cadillac wallowed down the highway and shrank in the distance, we drove down the road after him, taking up a speed to keep him in sight.

Gus turned the Caddie left, down a dirt road ahead, and proceeded perpendicular to us, a plume of dust marking his position on the horizon. We pulled over and stopped before he had taken the turn.

On each side of the dirt road were two brick pillars marking the entrance to the SUCCESS CENTER, the words written in iron script on one of them. There was no barrier across the road, no gate to close. Gus had left a plume of pinkish-brown dust hanging in the still afternoon, his car no longer visible, gone over the distant rise.

"Must be it. Now what?" asked Harouk. We both looked at Neffie. She shut off the motor to the El Camino and looked toward the center.

"Nez, would you be willing to reconnoiter?"

"I suppose. What do you want me to find out?"

"Go in and get some idea of the way the place is laid out. If you can meet Gus, find out where his office is, all the better. Go in as a visitor, look around, maybe buy some writings. Then come back and we can figure out what to do next."

Neffie and Harouk got out of the car and closed both doors.

"You want me to take the car and leave you here?" I looked up and down the highway. There was not another car in sight, just the desert. This go-in-and-look-around-plan felt half-baked. "Where will I meet you?"

"Don't worry about that. When you've worn out your welcome and found out all you can on this visit, go back to the service station. We'll find you there."

The two of them backed away from the car, waiting for me to drive off. I hesitated.

"This is a little loose, though. What do I say? What is the Success Center, anyway?"

"Don't worry. It will all become clear," said Harouk.

It will all become clear? This was a little too twinkle-

twinkle for me. Now I *was* worried. Neffie and Harouk were communicating in the same way they had when I had first met Harouk at her house near the diner. They had an unspoken bond between them, a way of working together that shut out everything else in a way that made it impossible to join in on what they were thinking unless one understood some hidden language. They had a plan, an agenda, they weren't telling me about. My reconnaissance might help that out, but what they were really doing was telling me to go play at the center for a while and they would catch up with me later, when they needed me.

There was, of course, nothing I could do about this. I wasn't about to say, "Hey, now wait just a doggone minute," so I nodded my consent, sincere but puzzled, and drove down the road, leaving them standing on the highway. "It will all become clear." Gimme a break.

The road to the center was a single-lane dirt path created more by the travel of cars than by any road-making equipment. The two ruts wriggled beneath the car, making the El Camino swish from side to side. There were no rocks, so the ride was free of jolts and I was able to make pretty good time. After a mile or so the road dipped through a shallow arroyo and when I came up the other side I saw the center. It was magnificent—white buildings set like a cluster of crystals next to huge red boulders. The complex was large and inviting with the road ending in a sweeping, paved circular drive in front of the entrance. Off to one side of the driveway was a parking lot with two-dozen cars. I didn't see Gus's car anywhere as I pulled into one of the spaces and stopped.

The center was clearly open to the public. There were

no guards, only two gardeners tending the rock and cactus gardens surrounding the buildings. The buildings looked as if they were designed in the sixties and had a strange beauty to them. Let me not underemphasize *strange*.

The center had a lot of the fast-food restaurant dynamic about it, but in addition to this wacky sentiment there was an element of high, thoughtful design. The large overhang of the roof resting on glass walls was not displeasing to the eye.

It was the arrangement of the buildings that was most salutary, as if crystals had begun growing from the base of the rock, the long horizontal crystals expressed by the main building, the vertical ones by a spire angling upward from a large auditorium-type of structure.

As I got out of the car I noticed another wonderfully exotic element of the compound. To the north, in a large, clear, desert area, was a landing strip, paved, probably one-hundred-fifty feet wide and four-thousand feet long. A wind sock luffed lazily above a small group of three well-maintained buildings I supposed were hangars.

I walked up the angled, shallow, flagstone steps to the main entrance of two floor-to-ceiling glass doors with immense handles made of dried ocotillo. Inside was a large, unattended reception desk on a polished granite floor. The desk, like something from an evening news broadcast, sat in the center of an atrium, rising above the main roof into a portico.

To one side was a saddle-colored leather bench, next to it a stand holding tiers of written material, pamphlets I recognized from the diner. I paced in the foyer for a few seconds, looking up and down the hallways, but saw no one.

Finally I sat down on the leather bench and picked up one of the pamphlets, *How to Extinguish a Cobalt Fire*. I was thumbing absentmindedly when I heard squishy footsteps.

I looked up to see a lovely woman, in her early sixties, with long gray hair, tan and wrinkled skin around clear blue eyes, and a warm, open smile. She was wearing a white muumuu cinched around her waist by a conch belt and leather sandals with rubber soles. She walked up to me and stood close, looking directly into my eyes. Then she took my hand, closed both of hers around it, and drew it toward her breast, pressing it into her solar plexus as she patted it.

I tossed the pamphlet I was holding onto the couch and smiled what may have been the weakest smile of my life. I didn't break contact, but my mind raced through all my possible escape scenarios. She stood there looking deep into my eyes like a psychic for what seemed like a week, then spoke.

"Hello. Thank you for coming to the center. How can I help you?" She released my hand. I released my breath.

She walked to the leather bench, sat down, and patted the place next to her.

"I'm Monica Humm. I'm sorry I wasn't here when you came."

I sat down next to her and she moved close to me, encroaching enough into my personal space to make me uncomfortable. And again she stared, unblinking, a cross between a gunfighter waiting for a move and a lunatic focusing somewhere just in back of my eyes.

She was pleasant enough to get away with this. The question I had was how long she could keep it up. I was assuming at some point she would return to normal and the usual social-dance areas would open between us. I was hoping, anyway.

"Actually Monica, I'm just looking around. I saw the sign and was intrigued so thought I would stop in." So far, so good. Nothing in that I couldn't adjust to the circumstance.

"Intrigued is a good place to start. Are you familiar with the Rootliff writings?" She said the phrase like *"was I familiar with the Rosetta Stone?"*

"Not really. I've seen a few in some restaurants."

"Then you have a wonderful new world ahead of you." She stood. I stood. "We have an energy center here for our residents and visitors. Would you like to share the evening energy with us?"

I felt the bag LittleHorse had given me shift in my pocket and remembered the magic stone that would break the magic windows. This place was floor-to-ceiling magic windows.

"That would be nice," I said. Then for the fun of it I tossed in, "I'm feeling a little formless right now," wondering how she would handle that nonsense.

She smiled a big at-last-we-have-connected smile. "And does your formlessness have a name?" she asked.

What? Wow, she was fast. That was even more screwy than my remark. "Oh, yeah. Sorry, Monica. My name is Nez."

"Ah. Very Zen."

"Backwards, actually." I smiled an I'm-making-a-joke smile.

We walked down one of the long hallways that radiated outward from the foyer. Down each hall were doors to classrooms. At the end of the hall we stepped outside into a long arbor covered with grapevines and wisteria and walked down it to an outdoor eating area, tables and benches arranged in cafeteria style around an outdoor flagstone fire pit. People were converging in the space from other arbors. They were dressed similarly, all in white except for some pieces of Indian jewelry.

They were almost lovely people, polished, seemingly serene, but with an unseeable high-frequency vibration to them, a tension. Was it sexual? Maybe. I kept smiling back at all the people that smiled at me, but not for the same reasons. I was thinking about why all utopias have such goofy clothing designers, a fly in the ointment if there ever was one. In the meanwhile, I was keeping my eyes open for some ideas about the layout of the compound.

"Monica, I hadn't planned on staying, or, really, eating. Is there a . . . how much is the dinner?"

"Five hundred dollars."

Five hundred dollars?! I said nothing, nodding instead.

"Well, I can't really make that level of commitment. I thought maybe I could get to know a little more about the place and whatever . . ."

"That's fine. You can stay here and watch the other people eat. You might want to ask them a question or two." She picked up a glass and clanged it with a spoon. "Everyone!"

"Everyone, listen! This is Nez. He's going to be watching us during this evening's energy. He says he was intrigued with the sign."

This caused a pockmark of applause and some loony laughter. I wanted to strangle Monica but fingered the stone in the little bag instead. Monica motioned for me to sit down on one of the benches. As I sat, everyone else sat down too. My discomfort was indescribable. I was sure someone was going to suggest we all play charades.

I didn't get an accurate count but I think there were between twenty and thirty people all gathered around. From a kitchen door to the side of the eating space came four waiters with covered trays, which they set about uncovering and serving. They were having rosemary chicken and some exotic undersea vegetable.

I was sitting next to a man, probably in his early thirties. Across from me was a short woman, next to her a tall, thin woman. I didn't think I was going to make it. I started to breathe fast.

"Are you going to stay for the lecture?" the skinny one asked as she tore the flesh from the bone of the rosemary chicken, making a little smack between *stay* and *for.*

"I don't know. I didn't. . . ."

"Mr. Rootliff is lecturing tonight," said Monica. "Tonight is the night we meet the new advanced *ungerret* class."

I kept my head down and glanced furtively at the food around me. In front of me was nothing. Finally I broke. I almost threw the bench over backwards as I stood up. Everyone on the bench with me grabbed the table at the same time, rattling the dishes and wadding the tablecloth in their clenched fingers.

"Sorry . . . I, uhh . . . Monica, I . . ." I choked, struck dumb. I managed to squeeze out the words, "Where is the men's room?"

"I'll show you," she said, as she abandoned her food and stood.

We walked away from the table and down a different

arbor. About halfway down the length of it were two bath-rooms. Monica pointed them out to me.

"Can you find your way back all right?" she asked.

"I have a compass and a map," I said. Monica stared blankly, then turned and walked away.

Inside the bathroom I splashed handful after handful of cold water on my face, letting it dribble down my clothes. I looked at myself in the mirror and checked to make sure nothing was showing, no telltale sign I was snooping, or worse, about to break into peals of nervous laughter.

I was staring in the mirror when Rootliff walked in. He looked at me in the mirror. I froze. Would he recognize me? He smiled faintly and kept going into the toilet stall. I dried my hands, went back outside, down the arbor to the tables and sat down again next to Monica. The young man next to me spoke.

"Have you started on the plan?" He was losing his hair and had begun an almost imperceptible comb-over.

"I'm sorry?" I said.

"I'll bet he's 'intrigued,' aren't you, Nez?" Monica held her hands up to make air quotes around the word *intrigued*.

"What is the plan?" I asked the man. He had a poolside tan and a mild rash on his forehead. Since he had missed a few spots while shaving, a small clump of one-day beard was growing below his left eye.

"Golly. You *are* just getting started," the short woman across the table said.

Suddenly everyone stood up. I turned around to see Root-liff walking into the courtyard. He waved them all to be seated.

"That's Mr. Rootliff. He runs the center" Monica said conspiratorially.

Mr. Rootliff walked to one side of the enclosure and stood behind a single microphone on a stand. He fairly shouted.

"Hi, winners!"

"Hi, Mr. Rootliff!" everyone shouted back.

Then he began speaking with the energy of an Amway sales motivator.

"Tonight, we are going to meet some of the new graduates of advanced *ungerret*. I've been working with these gals and believe me, you will love 'em. I'm gonna give you all a little talking-to tonight as well, so be sure to come right over to the auditorium right after evening energy. I see we have a visitor, and I want to invite you to come along too, friend. And like every other night, don't forget to . . ." he gave a pause and looked at the crowd patronizingly, waiting for them to finish the sentence, which they all did in unison.

". . . *bring your wallet!*"

Then everyone laughed and clapped as Rootliff waved everyone good-bye. A few of the people came up to Rootliff and began talking to him as the rest sat down.

"Is there a charge for the lecture?" I asked Monica.

Monica looked at the people sitting around like "we know something you don't know," then said, "Why don't you tell him, Lucille?"

Lucille was the skinny one next to the short one. She had a resemblance to Cruella de Vil. in the Disney cartoon *101 Dalmatians*, except she had no makeup on and one eye was ever so slightly crossed. Her long, jet-black hair was streaked with gray and, I was sorry to notice, a flake or two of dandruff. Her ears were bright red.

"Well, the advanced *ungerret* students are allowed to demonstrate the advanced *ungerret* privately, one-on-one, to the members of the advanced success seminars. See, here we have all graduated from Augie's—I mean Mr. Rootliff's—course on success so we all have more money than we need, and Mr. Rootliff's teaches us how to cycle the money energy to create more. So we buy things at the center to show our success. The private advanced *ungerret* is one of the most popular programs."

"How much does it cost?" I held my breath.

"Three thousand dollars," Monica said. Everyone at the table looked at me, expressionless. I didn't flinch.

"Really?" I said. "That may be a little stiff for me."

Somewhere in the distance I heard an unusual noise, unusual for the middle of the desert. It was a high whine getting closer and louder. In addition to the whine, I heard the muffled squeal of what could only have been a turboprop airplane. As the sound increased, covering all conversation, a Piagget Avanti, twin engines idling down for landing, blasted over the heads of the diners, all of whom turned to look.

The plane had caused a bit of a stir, but everyone quickly returned to finishing their meal and normalcy. Everyone, that is, except Augie Rootliff, whose face had gone white at the appearance of the plane, and who now dashed quickly from the room in a move I recognized as blind panic.

8

I TRIED TO THINK OF SOME REASON TO GET UP AND follow him, but could think of nothing, having used up the bathroom diversion.

Most of the members in the dining area were finished and were leaving in twos and threes. The people around me all left, except for Monica, who made it clear she was going to be my escort while I was in the place, either because she was afraid to leave me alone or because of some misdirected notion about enlisting me in the nonsense.

"And what brings you to this part of Arizona?" she asked, as the waiter cleared the table.

I had known she was going to ask that, but was lost for an answer. I was not about to say I'm trying to find out more about the legend of Neftoon Zamora and the magical city of Chuchen, to tell her about the blues tape. My mind was racing when, like a ball stopping on a wheel of fortune, I blurted, "I'm looking for UFOs."

Something about the moment, the place, the wacky look in Monica's eyes—I don't know why—it just came out. It could not have been more perfect, though, because somewhere inside the crazy-lady look of Monica Humm I had hit the jackpot. If she was doing chores around the Success Center to earn her keep, what brought her here was a search for spacecraft—that was her main agenda. The most remarkable look passed over her and all of her body language

155

shifted into a new syntax, her physiognomy cycling from benefactor-guide to naive hopeful. She handled it well, I thought, given that I was sure she wanted to throw herself into my arms and shriek, "At last, I found you!"

"Really? How long have you been interested in extra-terrestrial phenomena?"

I never heard it put quite that way. While I was cheerful about the connection between Monica and myself, I was a little troubled she would soon find out I knew nothing of UFOs and had practically no interest in them at all.

"For years now," I said. "I got interested when I was I child. I saw one once."

It was a wild hip shot, as crazy as the first remark and even more difficult to back up, but I thought, "As long as I'm out here this far I might as well look around, enjoy myself, see where this goes."

"I see," Monica said, uncrossing her ankles and spreading her legs so she could squeeze in closer to the table, leaning over, resting her chin on both of her closed hands, and looking longingly into my eyes. "What was it like?"

Oh, brother. Now what?

"I'm not sure, Monica. I was young and it's only a vague memory. I've probably been influenced by a lot of the things I've seen on TV and in the movies."

"I know what you mean. I saw one once when I was young. It landed."

I was beginning to feel bad. I didn't want to engage this woman in a complete hoax about something she obviously took seriously. I thought about some type of retreat. She brushed her hair back from her eyes and became thoughtful, then took a strand of hair, drew it across her mouth and began chewing on it. After a second or two, she went on.

"I didn't get close enough to ever see anyone, but it changed my life forever."

"Why is that?" I asked as fast as I could, less interested in the answer and more interested in getting the topic back in her hands.

"Because it was the greatest love I ever felt. I have never forgotten it, and to be honest, it is one of the reasons I first came to the center. I was, like you, wandering the desert looking for UFOs, when I met August. When that spacecraft landed in the field where I was camping with the Girl Scouts, I felt a communication coming from inside the ship, telepathic, and it told me I had been chosen, and that my life was special. Was yours anything like that?"

"No, not really. Mine was more, uh, mythological. As a matter of fact, I am not sure I ever really saw one."

"Oh, you mustn't let yourself think that way. Of course you saw one. Why else would you be here? Why would you be telling me this now, if it were not to fulfill a promise, a connection set by destiny?"

I decided to try the old switch-up.

"How long have you been at the center?"

"The center has only been here for twelve years, but I met August when I was in my twenties. He had a place near here. He was one of the few people who really listened to me and he taught me many things about life. I have helped him out over the years, all the way from calming some of the new girls to helping him set up new courses."

One thing was getting clear about Monica. She was genuine. I could see beneath her bag-lady potential she was a sweet and good person, even if she was a little light.

"But August doesn't really share my thinking about UFOs. He hasn't had the experience. You have, so you know what it's like to see one, to know they exist, but it's hard to talk sincerely with those who have not."

"I know what you mean," I said.

We stood up from the table and the change I had noticed was still present with Monica. She was treating me much more like a soul mate and less like a customer.

"There's an overlook where you can watch Armando's airplane take off. Would you like to see that?"

"Armando?" I said.

"Someone August works with. He has very nice planes. They come in once or twice a month, and all his planes are pretty." She motioned for me to come with her.

We walked along an outdoor path to the foot of the great red boulders that served as backdrop to the center, then along a sandy path to a high clearing that gave a clear view of the landing strip.

The Avanti, beautiful indeed, had started one of its twin pusher engines and still had the door open. From one of the hangars came three men and Rootliff. There was tension in the air.

"Hmm. That's funny," said Monica. "August didn't tell me he was leaving."

There was something more to her remark than curiosity; she was concerned. The other engine started up as everyone boarded and closed the door.

"He was supposed to give a lecture tonight and bring out the new girls. I wonder where he's going."

The plane taxied to the end of the runway and took off. Monica watched it with what I took to be a growing fear.

She made an effort to continue the tour.

"This is where I come at night sometimes and watch the stars, the skies. The landing strip seems friendly to me. I think sometimes I might see another . . ." she trailed off, preoccupied. "I'm sorry, Nez. I should go back in and see what happened to August. This is so unusual for him. He's never left in Armando's plane before. You're welcome to stay if you'd like. I'll send one of the other members to show you around."

"No. I understand, Monica. You sure there isn't something I can do to be helpful?"

"Thank you, nothing. I'm sorry not to be more hospitable."

We started back down the path to the center, and when we came to the walkway to the main building Monica turned and offered her hand in a proper handshake.

"If you take this walkway around the side, just here," she said, pointing around the outside of the building, "it will take you back to the parking lot. I hope you'll come back. I'd like to talk to you some more about our visitors from the stars. Don't lose faith in what you saw." She gave my hand a formal, perfunctory pump as she squeezed it, then hurried away.

I was standing alone outside the center. I could only get back to the main building if I went down the same path Monica had taken. I didn't want to do that. If I was caught, the impudence would be hard to explain. I looked around for another entrance to the building but didn't look too long before my own discomfort overtook me. I was not cut out for spy work. I decided to take Monica's instructions back to the parking lot and walked slowly along the flagstone walkway, looking at the beautiful cactus and rock. All were darkening in the incipient indigo of gathering twilight, while at the same time rimmed with the light orange from the setting sun. Suddenly, I heard Harouk.

"Nez." He was standing in the rock garden partially hidden from view behind a saguaro.

"Harouk. How did you get in here? I thought you were going back to the station."

Neffie walked up behind him.

"Did you get a look around?" Harouk said, avoiding my question.

"No. I went to something they call 'evening energy,' met some of the guests that are staying here, and Monica, the—I don't know—the madam, or concierge, or something. I never got off the main paths. Did you see the plane that came in and left?"

"Gus is on it," said Neffie. "I was watching. The men he was with were taking him somewhere he did not want to go."

"How long have you been here?" I was trying to reconcile the time I had been at the center with the time I thought it would have taken them to walk from the highway.

"Did she, Monica, give you any idea where he was going?" she said, bypassing the question as Harouk had.

"No, but she was upset about it. She left me here a few minutes ago. She thinks I'm leaving."

"And no sign of Kweethu?" Harouk said.

"At least not at 'evening energy.' " The three of us began walking to the parking lot.

160

"We need to find out where Gus went," said Neffie.

The outdoor lights began popping on from the photo-sensor switches as twilight settled in. The fragrance of sage brushed the air. We were at the parking lot, standing next to the El Camino.

Suddenly three men came out of the front doors and hurried quickly along one of the walkways, urgent, searching.

"Looks like Gus has been kidnapped," Neffie said. "That's a search party if I ever saw one. Can you ask Monica where the plane might have gone?"

"I can, but she's going to think it's weird. She thinks I'm looking for UFOs. . . ." As I said this, Neffie and Harouk looked behind me and signaled for me to be quiet.

I turned to see Monica approaching. She was simmering with anxiety, too absorbed to notice Neffie and Harouk until she was almost on us. Once she was aware of them she slowed slightly, but was overcome with worry and pressed on toward us.

"Hello," she said to the three of us.

"Monica this is, uh, Mary and Joe." I have no idea why I lied about their names. Just more spylike I guess. "They're friends of mine I was going to meet at . . ."

Monica didn't need any explanations. She nodded an indifferent hello to them. Harouk extended his hand and Monica shook it.

"Joe," said Harouk, "short for Jor-El, Superman's dad."

I wanted to kick him. He had thrown us into that nutty moment when I knew if I made any eye contact with him I would double over with laughter, and if I did that, the consequences would be dire, since the laughter would be unexplainable to Monica.

161

"Oh, you must be very proud," Monica said.

I looked at her for a split second, utterly confused. Fortunately, there was a glint in her eye. She was being facetious. Maybe this was her way of letting off tension, a little light laughter. That gave me the opening to laugh out loud with a purpose, which I did, letting the laughter blow off the tension like the steam whistle on a ship. But it was not to be a good, long laugh because Monica only smiled and quickly returned to her seriousness, to her anxiety.

"Nez, when August left, did you notice whether he was carrying anything, a suitcase or a bag?"

"I really didn't."

Monica's brow furrowed. I felt bad for her. She seemed on the verge of hysteria. A tremble was slowly overtaking her, starting with her hands. Neffie stepped in.

"Are you worried about something?" she asked.

That was all Monica needed. She began to wring her hands and to talk while struggling for composure.

"I think August is in trouble. Serious trouble. Those men on the plane were from Nevada."

She said the word *Nevada* like she might have said *Beelzebub*.

"What do you think has happened to him?" Neffie probed further.

"I don't . . . I really shouldn't bother you with this."

"If we can help, Monica, we will." When Neffie said that, she sounded like Monica's guardian angel. I didn't understand how she had managed to shift from our mission of finding Kweethu to helping Monica retrieve Rootliff, but the sincerity was real, undeniable. Monica surrendered. The tears flowed as Neffie walked to her and put her arms around her in a display of comfort and affection that was inspiring.

"I'm afraid they may hurt him," Monica said through tears.

"Let's go somewhere we can talk." Now Neffie was in full command.

Monica nodded and motioned for us to follow her. As we walked to the main entry and down one of the halls, the three men I had seen earlier walked up to Monica. They were not interested in us. One of them spoke.

"He's not here."

Monica nodded to him. "Okay. I was certain I saw him leave with the fellows from the plane. Okay. Thank you for looking. John, tell the members there will not be a lecture tonight and handle the advanced *ungerret* yourself, will you? It's four thousand."

There is something to be said for maturity. If Monica had been a younger person I think she would have not had the presence of mind to keep the activities of the center going. I was impressed with her aplomb.

We continued through the complex until we came to what could only have been Gus's office.

It was a large rectangular room with a fireplace along one wall and a glass partition to an enclosed garden at one end. A desk was catty-corner at the other end, in front of it a conversational seating area of a sofa and two easy chairs around a low table. The table was piled high with books and papers as was his desk—messy. The walls were covered with pictures of various people with Gus, a large white board with some recent scribbling, and a framed poster of "Seven Sacred Sayings of Success." I didn't read them but noticed in passing there seemed to be only six. Monica motioned for us to sit down in the chairs and sofa, which we did as she went behind Gus's desk and picked up a small piece of paper. I thought it must be some kind of ransom note, perhaps a suicide note, or good-bye letter, because she held it away from her like it had an odor, holding it by her thumb and forefinger at arm's length and turning her head slightly from it. She brought it to Neffie and handed it to her.

"I found this on his desk. Gus has been having some trouble, I think, meeting some payment schedules. The men in the plane usually come once a week and leave in a few minutes with a briefcase. This is the first time he's gone with them. It isn't like him to go like this, without saying anything. He's been talking about flying to Nevada but . . . he just came back from New Mexico and was really afraid. He said he had been unable to get the money back from someone who had taken it."

I looked surreptitiously at Harouk and raised my eyebrows. He nodded ever so slightly.

"When he came back was anyone with him? A woman, an Indian woman?"

"No," said Monica, a little curious Neffie would ask such a pointed and informed question. "Why?"

"We knew the man Gus went to see in New Mexico," Neffie said.

Monica looked at all of us without speaking, somewhere between fright and puzzlement.

"Do you know Gus?" she asked, trying to understand who we were.

"No, we had never seen Gus, until he showed up where we worked. He had a gun and he started shooting."

"Oh my god," Monica said. "And you people are the police."

We shook our heads in unison.

"No, no. We aren't after Gus. But a friend of ours was with him and she has disappeared. Gus picked her up in Quemado and was the last person we know she was with."

"Oh, dear god," Monica said, now really succumbing to some horror she had in her mind. "I knew he was in trouble."

"Maybe, maybe not," said Neffie. "Did he say anything about his trip to New Mexico?"

"Only that he couldn't get the money back, someone had stolen it, and he was concerned Armando would be extremely angry and do something."

"Armando?" Harouk said.

"He's the man who lent Gus the money to build the center. They have all sorts of dealings, but I never was sure what they were." She pointed to the note she had handed Neffie. "What do you suppose this means? It's frightening to me."

Neffie studied it, then showed it to Harouk. Both of them were mystified, as if looking at some recondite, obscure language. They handed it to me. I recognized it immediately. It was a flight plan.

"This is a flight plan," I said. "You said Gus was planning to go to Nevada?"

Monica nodded yes.

A flight plan is a routine document pilots use to inform the air-traffic system about a proposed flight. This was a VFR

165

flight plan to a latitude and longitude coordinate, probably a private field. Without a map I couldn't tell where it was, only that it was somewhere in the Southwest.

"Do you know where Gus keeps his flight gear?" I asked.

"No. He usually wears his regular clothes when he goes flying."

"No, I mean maps and stuff like that. Pilots usually carry a bag with maps and airport directories, things like that. Where might that be?" I asked.

"It's most likely in the plane."

"Can we take a look?" I asked. "Just to ease your mind, this is nothing sinister." I held up the paper. "I think I can tell where Gus is from this."

"Okay." Monica stood and led us out of the room. As we walked, Neffie put her arm around Monica and said something quietly to her. Monica nodded and smiled in appreciation.

I was walking beside Harouk.

" 'Superman's dad'?" I said.

"She thought it was funny. It was good for the moment." Harouk was deadpan.

I gave him a shove on the shoulder.

We walked from the complex along the outdoor winding paths down a few steps to the hangars. Monica dialed in a combination on one of the doors, opening it to reveal a beautiful early-eighties V Tail Bonanza.

Neffie, Harouk, and Monica stood beside the plane while I climbed in and looked around for Gus's pilot bag. It was on the backseat. I took out two of the aeronautical charts and laid them out on a table set against one wall of the hangar. It was the first time I had understood exactly where I was, at least according to a map.

The Success Center was south of the Apache National Forest, southeast of the towns of Stargo and Morenci, near the junction of the Eagle Creek and the Gila River. Gus had a flight plan that took him into northern Nevada between Elko and Battle Mountain to a private strip somewhere near Newmont Mine in the Tuscarora Mountains, a low range of five- and six-thousand-foot peaks. Whether this was where Gus had gone with the men in the Avanti was another story.

"Did Gus ever tell you where Armando lived? Did he ever mention the name of a town?" I asked Monica.

"Oh, if he ever did I never paid any attention."

"The flight plan takes him here." I pointed to the chart. "Do any of these towns ring a bell?" Monica read the map and shook her head no.

"Can you fly this?" Neffie asked me.

"Sure," I said.

Neffie turned to Monica. "Do you think we should go look for him?" she asked.

"I don't know. Maybe. Could you really get there?" Monica asked me.

I recognized the question as more than what was said. I had answered it many times before. The question was really, won't this thing plummet to the ground if you have the slightest problem, can one really navigate the skies, if god had meant for man to fly wouldn't he have given us wings, aren't airline pilots a cross between genius-level physicists and supercomputing robots? All this rolled into the questioning look now in everyone's eyes except Neffie's.

"If you would like me to fly us to the destination on

this flight plan I can do that easily, assuming this is an airworthy ship.''

"Oh, Gus kept it in perfect shape" said Monica. "But . . .''

I didn't like any equivocation in a statement like this one.

"But what?" I said.

"Maybe you three could go. I wouldn't want to leave the center.''

Monica's instinct for trust was amazing to behold. I had the feeling it put a panoply of protection around her, so complete was her faith in the goodness of other people. She was willing for the three of us to leave with Gus's airplane and she had no doubt we would go forth and return faithful to the task of finding Gus, and not simply steal the airplane. The astounding thing, the lovely thing, that made the childlike trust of Monica Humm so startlingly substantial, was that she was absolutely right. That is exactly what we would do.

It was then I noticed Harouk. He was not happy. Some people have an aversion to flying—in fact, most people do—then some are categorically, unequivocally, sincerely terrified. Harouk was one of these. I could see it in his eyes, darting from escape to escape, looking for cover. Whatever else might happen tonight, Harouk was never going to set foot in this aircraft.

The little kid in me thought about saying, "C'mon Harouk, this airplane used to fall apart in the sky, but it's fixed now." Instead, I opened an escape for him. I didn't want him to have to explain himself.

"We can go look, Monica, but it might be best if one

of us stayed here, to help you keep an eye on things, and we have our car here, so . . ." It was lame, but it was the best I could come up with as far as giving Harouk a flight-preempting job.

"I can stay," Harouk said with remarkable restraint. "Fine with me. I'll watch the car."

Monica walked to a metal locker next to the table we were gathered around, opened it and took a set of keys off a hook inside.

"These are to the plane. How long will it take you to get there?"

I looked at the flight plan.

"About three hours if all goes well."

I looked at the wind sock above the building. The wind was directly down the runway, blowing gently. I grabbed a tow bar leaning against the wall, wrestled the airplane out of the hangar, and pointed it into the wind. The stars were out now and I could see a faint halation along the distant horizon heralding a moonrise. Neffie turned to Harouk.

"Turn your phone on just in case. What's the number here?" she asked Monica.

Monica wrote the phone number for the center on the map I was using.

I began a preflight exam of the Beech, and when I was sure we were ready to go, climbed in the pilot's seat. Whatever Gus's shortcomings, they were not apparent in his airplane. Everything looked in excellent condition. Neffie got in after me and sat next to me in the right-hand seat.

Harouk and Monica stood by each other next to the hangar, watching as this most abnormal of human activities got underway. The relief on Harouk's face was palpable, the hope on Monica's touching. I gave them a little wave as the motor started and we taxied to the end of the runway. Then I checked behind us, gave the little butterfly full power and we lifted off into the night sky. I made a climbing right turn and crossed the landing strip at about five hundred feet. Below we could see the tiny figures of Harouk and Monica, eyes skyward, as they waved us good fortune.

9

W E CLIMBED OUT AT EIGHT-HUNDRED FEET PER MIN-
ute and I contacted the Phoenix flight services to open the
flight plan, using Elko as my destination, got the weather,
which was clear, then requested "flight following," a way
of keeping the airplane under watch by the flight center.

"UFOs?" Neffie said when I was off the radio.

"What?"

"You told Monica you were looking for UFOs?" she
asked again.

"How did you know that?"

"When we were walking to the plane. She asked me if
we were only looking for our friend or were we looking
for UFOs as well."

"Oh no," I said, not wanting Monica to feel hurt. "And
you said . . . ?"

"I said I thought you had seen one once and that it was
always on your mind a little, but I wasn't sure." She turned
to me with a slight questioning arch in her eyebrow.

"Remarkable. That's exactly what I said—I was looking
for spacecraft, but when she lit up, desperate for the connection, I knew I had opened the wrong door. I mean, this
is no casual interest for her. I kept retreating until I said
something like I probably never saw one, but by then she
wouldn't let it go. She told me to hang on to the dream.
She was sure I saw one. I'm glad you took care of her."

"She needed it. To dispose of things, if nothing else. She's a good woman. I wonder if Gus knows that." Neffie gazed out the window.

A three-quarter moon had risen into the heavenly dome. The light gave the land below a silken sheen of gray velvet and the planet stretched out, clearly visible. One of the worries of night flying is not being able to see the horizons, but tonight that would be no problem. Once we were at altitude I picked up a heading to our next waypoint and switched on the autopilot. The plane was well-equipped with plenty of first-class radio and navigation equipment.

"Did you ever see a UFO?" Neffie asked.

"Not so's you'd know. I've seen some unexplained lights in the sky, and I've seen a few unusual things when I've been flying, but hardly what I'd call UFOs. The thing that got to me about Monica was the life-altering aspect of her sighting. I have no doubt she saw something; what, I don't know, but the compelling element is her report of this telepathic communication with a benevolent being and her feeling of peace and, as she said, indescribable love. It's like she wanted or needed something so much she created an instrument to bring it into her life."

"One of the Zamora legends has spaceships," she said.

"I'm not surprised."

"In Chuchen, thousands of years after the first legend, the one when Neftoon saved all the people from the wolves, there was another incident.

"Do you remember the young boy Zamora gave the flute to, and the berry seeds? He was to become known as Kokopelli in the tales of the Anasazi. The story goes he lived for over a thousand years, like some of the main figures in the Old Testament, and that he traveled about, planting seeds not only of berries and other plants, but also having many children.

"At the time of this legend, Chuchen was a city of several thousand people and Kokopelli was the father of the chief of Chuchen. So, when Kokopelli would visit, there was always a big celebration, the chief would turn out the finest food, and there would be a party for five days and nights. Fortunately, Kokopelli came but once a year.

"The legend of Black Wolf was passed along during these festivals and Kokopelli always emphasized the ending, explaining that Neftoon had sacrificed herself for the good of the tribe.

"As the years went on, this notion of sacrifice became more and more perverted, until the chief began to use it to his own ends. Sacrifice, he taught, must involve the offering of one of the young women of Chuchen to the goddess Zamora. This offering included virginal sex with the chief, then the death of the young girl by tossing her over a cliff. Since the chief chose the girl, he held the little village in fear, ruling more and more absolutely because he controlled life and death among them. It was taught that sacrifice to Zamora kept the tribe from harm and insured prosperity, so it was an honor to be the sacrificial offering, an honor to everyone but the one being sacrificed.

"Things got worse. A general malaise descended on the people once a year as they all wondered who was going to get sacrificed, as they sank deeper and deeper into the belief the only way happiness and the well-being of the village could be assured was to kill one of their children.

"One particular year, the young girl who was chosen

for the sacrifice decided she would not go along with this madness, and ran away. She was only twelve years old, so the grown-ups quickly overtook her, cornering her in a small ravine. They picked her up, tied her, and threw her over the back of a donkey and brought her back.

"When they got to town, they took the girl to the chief for the sacrificial sex but she simply wouldn't uncross her legs. She said they would have to kill her first. Then she cried out in anguish that if sacrifice, the destruction of something, was what made the world work, wouldn't they all be better off dead? Who would want to live in a world where life was made sacred by death?

"At that moment a great, golden vessel came from the sky and landed near the ceremonial site. Out stepped Neftoon Zamora, looking exactly the way she was described in the legends. The town was jubilant . . . and terrified. Since for years they had been killing people to get Zamora's blessings, they were happy to see they had finally gotten her attention. On the other hand, life had become a nightmare, for their life was ruled by death. This reality, they thought, lay directly at Neftoon's feet. Naturally they were worried. What new horror would she visit upon them?

"The first thing Zamora did was go to the altar built for the sacrifice of the young child, and let her loose. Then she turned to the people and told them that destroying someone was not sacrifice but a type of insanity, that the legend of Black Wolf had been perverted.

"She said the important part of the Black Wolf legend was understanding the power of intelligence over ignorance, the power of love over hate.

"Then she pointed to the ship and said the legend of her

sacrifice was like the spaceship. She cautioned them not to worship the spacecraft, but to see it as a symbol of the basic power of intelligence, organizing ideas in a way that was useful to them, that insured the perpetuation of order and harmony, that maintained life, instead of destroying it.

"There were by this time chief priests of the Zamora cult, and they questioned her. How, they asked, could such a terrible twist of her teachings have happened?

"She said it was because the nature of mortality was to destroy itself, so the man who accepted mortality as his selfhood would always see death as the only outcome of life. After that, she got in her spaceship and took off.

"The Chuchinas drove the chief from the village, tore down the alter, and reduced Kokopelli to a comical figure like the tooth fairy. Then they began to build Chuchen once more, this time with a new legend of Neftoon Zamora.

"And what do you think is the part of the story that has been most carefully preserved? Don't answer, I'll tell you. It's the spaceship part. There exist now elaborate descriptions of the spacecraft, paintings of it, sculptures of it, speculations and teachings about its drive mechanism, even detailed descriptions of writings and symbols purportedly on the outside of the ship. All of this combined with the idea Zamora was from another planet, way out of reach, and from time to time she might land and help out with things, or if we could only build a spaceship like hers we could make our way to Zamoraland, somewhere beyond the heavens. In South America there were even landing strips maintained in case she should ever return. Go figure."

We were nearing our destination and I was privately wishing for a spaceship with exceptional powers, since I was wondering how I was going to find a private field at night, moonlight or not. It's one thing to have a horizon to navigate by, another to try to find a little airport somewhere on the ground. I had Elko as an alternate if I couldn't find it, but I only had so much fuel. I could look around for about ten minutes, then we would have to land at Elko, something I was not looking forward to.

When I got over the field as shown on the flight plan, I decided to see if the runway had pilot-controlled lighting. This is a way for a pilot who needs it, to turn on any airport landing-strip lights remotely.

I tuned to a standard Unicom frequency and hit the mike switch three times in succession. It worked. Right below a fully-lit runway appeared. Lavishly lit in fact. It had the lighting system of a major airport, something you might see at LAX.

I made one pass over the runway but didn't know until I was down low whether it was paved or not, then a few hundred feet off the end I could see it was a good, hard surface in excellent condition. The runway must have been eight-thousand feet long, big enough and wide enough for commercial jets. As the wheels of the origami-butterfly plane chirped on the asphalt I noticed lights had gone on in some buildings at the end of the runway.

We rolled off to the side onto a parallel taxiway. More lights were coming on. It was a little after ten o'clock in the evening. I imagined we had woken someone up. I couldn't suppress my trepidation.

"This may not have been such a good idea. Maybe we should get back in the air right away," I said to Neffie. It was too late.

A small airport jeep pulled in back of the plane as another one pulled in front. I had not seen them until they were next to us. The one in front turned on a large FOLLOW ME sign on the back of the jeep. The men in the jeep behind us had M16 rifles and were holding them with the barrels straight up, the butts of the guns resting on the floor of the jeep, next to their boots.

The field was surrounded by a group of low mountain peaks. Ahead were the hangars and several airplanes. Inside the first hangar, off in a corner was a Lear fifty-five, dwarfed by the room, next to it a Pitts, a little bi-wing sports plane, then the Avanti I had seen at the center, next to it an A-Star helicopter, next to it a Gulfstream G Four, the status corporate airplane, and finally a Canadair Challenger 600, the more serious corporate jet, like a thirty-five-foot long 737, a real no-nonsense bird. The open door was revealing the interior light as it spilled out onto the tarmac. Behind it were two more huge hangars, each one well over fifty-thousand square feet. These people were into aircraft and had a lot of money.

From offices along the side of the hangar I saw four men in black jumpsuits appear, walking onto the hangar floor, watching the little Beech closely. The jeep in front of me drove into the hangar, one of the men jumped out of the right seat and motioned me forward with the usual ground-handling signals. At the last second, when I should have stopped, instead I did a ninety-degree turn and began to taxi away. The jeep that was behind us raced around toward the front of the plane and forced us off the tarmac into a dirt-and-gravel apron and finally blocked our path. The two men jumped out and held their guns at the ready.

177

The man who had been giving me ground signals before ran around to the front of the plane and began frantically drawing his hand across his throat in a gesture for me to shut down the engine.

I didn't like getting pushed around like this. Just for the hell of it, I revved the engine up to a high RPM. The two men with the M16s lifted the guns to their shoulder, ready to fire. I pulled the mixture knob to shut off and the engine died. I noticed with some degree of satisfaction I had kicked up a huge amount of debris and dust, which was settling over the big airplanes in the hangar in back of me. I hoped the gravel had damaged a few windscreens. I turned to Neffie and made a kind of "I couldn't help myself" face in apology for endangering us. She was calm.

"Well. Here we are."

More men began surrounding the plane. All of them were white, in black jumpsuits, with no markings, and all of them were big. Neffie and I crawled out of the plane. The oldest man came up to me. He was nodding a sardonic "I know your type of smart-ass" nod.

"Are you with Gus?" he asked.

"Yeah, well, I mean this is his plane." I decided to say nothing more. I looked the man straight in the eyes.

Then Neffie said, "Is he here?"

The older man, clearly the boss, looked at the rest of the team. I looked past him into the hangar and was pleased to see it was now filthy from the little butterfly's prop wash. One of the men was checking the intake of the Gulfstream's jets for dirt, a handful of which he found and held up in disgust for his boss to see. His boss was now glaring at me. I was expressionless. "You'll just have to deal with it, pal,"

I thought. I hoped it showed in my eyes, but was careful to give nothing away for free.

"Yes. Wait here, please."

He walked away and left Neffie and me standing there surrounded by seven men. No one said a word. The tension was so thick you could skate on it. After what seemed like a week, the boss signaled from the office. He was holding a phone. At this the seven men dispersed, leaving one young fellow. He was in his early twenties and looked like he was right out of the military police.

"Follow me, please."

We walked to the office at the side of the hangar, through it, and to the outside where the boss and one other man were sitting in a small gas-powered golf cart. He motioned curtly for us to get in.

The two jumpsuits sat in the front, Neffie and I in the back. In a movie, this was where we would have been blindfolded. We drove away from the hangar along a small paved road, barely wide enough for two of these little carts.

Riding behind the two men, I could look around unobserved by them. We were in the middle of a complex of large metal buildings, strictly utilitarian, lit by yellow-sodium arc lights. The buildings were surrounded by black asphalt, which disappeared after a few feet into a sandy terrain, some of which was now all over the inside of their pristine hangar, thanks to me. With the lights I could see something of the countryside, but not enough to tell the detail. What forms I did see were low hillocks and some peaks, made grotesque by the vapor lights. The roadway we were on turned away from the main buildings and into the desert, into the enveloping night.

Then, as we rounded the base of a hill I saw it, poised on top of one of the mountains: an enormous house, five stories high, occupying the entire top plateau, all sides of the house built to the edge of the mountaintop, which was the edge of a precipice. The house was twice as big as the hangar. It sat on the top of this mountain like a Bavarian castle, only without a hint of fantasy, the only ingress the road we were on.

The road curved up the side of the hill in a long series of s turns to an eight-foot-high solid gate that swung open on our approach. Extending out from the gate in both directions was an antipersonnel fence of staggering proportions, eight feet high and topped with rolls of razor wire. Approximately every ten feet along the perimeter was an outward-facing sodium floodlight, and from these one could see the power boxes that attached voltage to the fence.

Behind this fence, roughly twelve feet up the hill, was another eight-foot-high chain-link fence topped with razor wire as well. Between the two fences was gravel, freshly raked, and I imagined, covering some type of detection system should anyone stray into this terrible trap.

As we neared the main residence, I could see the building blocks comprising the house were all of one piece. This was not a group of buildings, but one giant edifice, of different levels and enclosures, a castle without turret, tower, or palisade. It was as if a suburban stucco home had swollen until it covered the mountaintop. Nowhere was there character of any type, no decoration, art, colors, attention to design— nothing but a faceless stack of boxes over thousands of square feet atop the mountain.

We came to a stop at a front door like the front door

to a tract home but twice the size. Faux brass handles over a machine-carved panel door. Ironically, in the center of the left-hand door was a small glass peephole of the type they provide in cheap motels. The door opened and we were greeted by Armando Hotchkiss.

Hotchkiss was disarmingly open. He was not smiling, but he was not frowning either. I felt as if he saw everything, that if he had been asked to describe the most minute detail of our clothing or mannerisms he could have done so perfectly. He was wearing a silk bathrobe and velvet monogrammed slippers.

I thought him to be in his late seventies or early eighties. An enormous pair of black-rimmed glasses covered a hawk-like, angular face, but he had a relaxed mouth and eyebrows. He seemed supremely confident and assured. The glasses had small panels on either side coming back along the stems, which filtered out the side light through small dark lenses, making the glasses look more like protective goggles than optometrics. The lenses, however, were clear, and his gaze drilled out from behind them, unwelcoming but unwary, an unusual combination.

Neffie and I got off the little cart, which drove away. We stood there waiting for Hotchkiss to make his opening. For a second his brow furrowed slightly. Then, quickly, he controlled his face again. He relaxed, but somewhere in the depths of his soul I was sure this man was encountering a threat and steeling himself against it.

I glanced at Neffie without turning my head. There was the slightest narrowing of her eyes. Something was up, all right. The air was cool, the skies were clear except for a distant, blue cold front of approaching clouds, the wind was dead calm, but I knew if I could only have been inside the heads of these two people I would have heard the clap of thunder and the roar of a gale, the clash of hostile powers.

"Why, if it isn't, I mean . . . you look exactly like . . . like Neftoon Zamora. My god. This is quite a night. Quite a night. Come in, come in."

I turned and looked at Neffie for some clue or insight into what was transpiring between her and Armando, but she only looked back and gave the slightest shrug of her shoulder. Whatever was between these two she was not going to reveal at that moment. We both followed him in. The foyer was precisely what the exterior had promised: a large entryway with nothing of distinction and not one decoration except for a hideous pot on a pedestal, a kind of shopping-mall decoration from hell.

He led us through several rooms of no apparent purpose, but gigantic nonetheless, until we finally came to a study and office. It was also colossal, with several seating areas. He sat at a round table encircled by four straight-back chairs, and motioned for us to do likewise.

"How did you get Gus's airplane? I'm sorry. I'm Armando Hotchkiss. How did you get Gussie's plane?" He was not interested in Neffie or me introducing ourselves to him.

"It's a bit unusual, but we were at the center when he left, and we think he may know where a friend of ours is, so . . ."

"What were you doing at the center? Are you a member?" He interrupted me.

"Good lord, no," I said. "I mean . . . uh . . . no offense, but, no. We were looking for someone Gus had with him when he came to Apache Springs.''

"I see. I see the connection. And you?" He turned to Neffie.

"I was at the diner," she said.

"Oh, of course. Of course you were . . . would have been." Hotchkiss had the deep back-story on Gus and the diner, this was becoming obvious, and there was more he knew about Neffie than he was showing.

"Is Gus here?" Neffie asked.

"He is, he is. Would you like me to wake him? Actually, no, let me take that back. It's late, I've been in bed an hour now. We actually should all be in bed. Is there anything that can't wait till the morning?"

"Yes. We need to know what happened to Kweethu. We think Gus kidnapped her and I want to know where she is," said Neffie, direct and tough.

"Kweethu? I . . ." Armando shook his head, then sighed in resigned annoyance. "All right then . . . I'll get him." He crossed to a desk that did not have one piece of paper on it and picked up a small handheld radio. "Tommy, can you wake Mr. Rutcliff? Have him come to the east study. Thank you." Armando turned to us. "He'll only be a minute or two. So you took his plane and followed him?"

"No," I said. "Wild hunch. He left a flight plan behind so we followed that."

Before anyone could say more, however, Gus walked in the room. This was not the man I had seen at the service station, not the master of ceremonies I had seen at the center. He was drastically and dramatically changed. It was almost as if his physical stature had shrunk. He was sweating profusely. The look in his eyes was intense as a cornered animal's. He may well have been wakened, but it looked to me more as if he had been unhooked from a noose, that he had been on the verge of something terrible and perhaps still was. Our sudden arrival had stopped whatever horror was afoot, but it looked as if Gus thought of this summons only as reprise, not salvation. When he saw Neffie, he turned pale and I thought he would faint.

"I believe you have a mutual friend with these people," Armando said to Gus.

Gus steadied himself by leaning against a chair. He was staring at Neffie and gave me only a quick glance.

"I know you," Gus said to Neffie. "You work at Li's Diner."

"That's right," Neffie said. "The one you shot up."

Gus looked at the floor, then back to her, then to Armando.

"I told you, Li was the one who stole the money," he said to Hotchkiss.

Hotchkiss shrugged, as if to say, so what?

"More to the point, Gus, what happened to Kweethu?" Neffie was at her full height.

"Who?" Gus was perplexed.

"Kweethu. You had her in the car with you."

"The old woman from Quemado? I took her back to Acoma, let her off at bingo."

The little kid had been right. She was playing bingo.

"When?" Neffie pressed him.

"After I came back from the diner. I had forgotten she was in the car. . . ."

"You forgot about her?" Neffie said.

"I offered her some money to take me to Li. In the . . . uh . . . excitement, I forgot about her, that's all. When she popped up in the backseat, she said she wanted me to take her to bingo at Acoma, Sky City Casino. So I did. That's the last I saw of her."

"You let her off, that was it?" asked Neffie.

"That was it," Gus said.

We all stood silent. Neffie looked at Gus for a long time, trying to convince herself of his honesty, I thought. At last Armando broke the silence.

"If that's all you need, can we all go to bed?"

Neffie turned to me. "We can call there, find out when she left, see how long she was there."

"You'll be happy to know they brought your airplane, Gus," Armando said.

I could see Gus was not happy about this at all.

"Here?" he said, surprised and a little miffed.

"Down in hangar two," Armando said.

"Who flew it?" Gus asked.

I was about to say something, but Armando was curt.

"Gentleman and lady . . . this meeting is over. I'm going to bed. You all will do the same, please. You can work out all mysteries tomorrow morning. Nothing more needs to be discussed tonight."

He pushed a button in his desk and almost instantly a young man entered the room, early twenties with a military haircut, thick neck and sloping shoulders. He stood, saying nothing, legs slightly apart, his hands folded in front of him.

"Tommy, show these people to their room. Are you two separate or together?"

Armando looked at Neffie. The question was deep, directed only at her.

"Together," Neffie responded.

"Fine. Show them the suite by the library. We will have a late breakfast. Good night."

With that, Armando held his hands out to herd us from his study. None of us said another word as Gus went off to the left, down a hallway, and Armando pressed a button for an elevator directly opposite the door to the study. As the door opened in front of him, Tommy, Neffie, and I started our walk down a long hallway, down a series of stairs, through some other tremendous rooms dotted with useless furniture, and finally to a suite of three rooms, a bedroom, bath, and dressing room. It was like a business hotel, no character, humanity, grace or charm in any of it. The only picture, above the bed, was a print, a picture of a house and its reflection in a lake; autumnal, purely decorative, perfunctory, nearly bucolic, simply awful.

"There are towels and bathrobes in the closet." He nodded his good night, closed the door and left. Immediately after he was gone I went to the door and tried the handle. It was open, so I pushed it outward and checked down the hallway. Tommy was about to turn a corner when he heard me and looked back.

"Did you need anything?" he asked, polite but distant.

"No, just . . . just checking," I said. "Thanks. Good night."

He continued around the corner.

"Well, we're not locked in," I said as I closed the door behind me.

I looked around the room. There was no phone, no

television, no books, nothing of ordinary life in a connected world. The room was like a cell. It was creepy. Most houses have a sentience, a personality, the evidence of which is the bric-a-brac, art, furniture design, a point of view. There was nothing like that here.

"There's a little basket of shampoo and lotions," Neffie said as she came out of the bathroom. "Like a motel."

"Yeah," I said. "The Bates."

"Probably more than we know," Neffie said as she bounced on the bed once, then stretched out.

I went into the bathroom to see the loot: four small bottles of toiletries, enough for one use. "What do you suppose he does?"

"I wouldn't know." Neffie yawned. "At least I have the feeling Kweethu is safe. I didn't get any negative hits off Gus, more like dopey hysteric." At that moment I realized Neffie had been analyzing Gus more for his relationship to Armando than for his involvement with Li and Kweethu. Not only was she sure Kweethu was safe, more importantly it seemed, she had decided Gus was inconsequential in any proceedings here at Armando's empty castle.

I sat on the edge of the bed.

"It makes sense. Kweethu has stayed at the casino for twelve straight days before. She won eighteen-hundred dollars once and that was it, she's played religiously ever since, bingo, blackjack, craps, whatever. It's sad. Who would have thought that the great wisdom of the Native Americans would turn out to be 'always split aces and eights'?"

"If she's safe, what now?" I tried not to let it show, but I was confused, far out of touch with my purpose in coming to the enchanted land. I wanted to find the source of an extraordinary music, to learn what I could about the artistry, perhaps to gain a bit in my practice as an artist. What was I supposed to learn here? I looked at Neffie on the bed, her gorgeous form; enticing, warm, comforting. The love that had overtaken me when I first met her and made love to her was transmuting. I felt different. What appealed to me now was her clearheaded strength, her capacity for calm in unusual circumstances. I had left my attachment to her as a possible life partner back in Welach. Perhaps it was for the best. I still loved her, but I was learning more about what that meant.

"We fly back with Gus. Unless you had something else in mind." Neffie propped her head up, resting her elbow on the bed.

Discomfort was crowding around me. Throughout my trip I'd had this nagging feeling of something not right, sometimes a free-floating anxiety, other times focused on specific peril, but always there, chipping away at my composure. It was rising this night, more corrosive than before. Usually I could shake it, turn my thoughts to more benevolent or comforting ideas, but tonight that wasn't working. It was fear, no doubt of that, but something underneath the fear, more hideous, a satanic, evil magnetism, sucking me by sections into a disorganization, into a universe uncontrolled, random, subject only to a malevolent caprice. Whatever Welach was, Armando's castle was the opposite. I wanted out, the sooner the better. Neffie knew this.

I crawled next to Neffie in the bed and turned my back to her as I drew one of the pillows to my chest and curled around it in a fetal position. I did not undress or pull the covers over me. Neffie settled too, but only after rubbing my arm, a loving caress. Some of the strength she possessed came through to me, calming me. Still, the abiding thought in my head was "I don't want to be here." I rolled over and looked deep into this woman's eyes and kissed her full and long on the mouth, drinking deeply of her soul. Whatever had brought me here had brought me Neffie too, and for that I would always be happy. I folded into her arms, where peaceful, dreamless sleep was only moments away.

10

I WOKE EARLY, JUST BEFORE DAWN. NEFFIE HAD SNUG-gled under the covers sometime during the night and was still wrapped in them. I moved as quietly as possible so not to disturb her, went to the bathroom and splashed water on my face and hair.

The window that had been dark the night before was now gray and drizzly with the opening day. I heard a plane and looked out in time to see the Canadair take off, followed in less than a minute by the Lear. A few more minutes passed and the Pitts took off. I saw them only seconds after they were airborne before they disappeared into the overcast. I couldn't see the runway or the hangars from my room.

I found a new toothbrush in a cellophane-wrapped box and some mouthwash in the bathroom. I had nothing with me for traveling, only the clothes I was wearing and had now slept in. I looked a mess, except I noticed there was no sign of injury left on my face. All was back to normal. Neffie did not stir.

I left the room, deciding to explore a little in the early-morning hours. As the light increased I could see more and more of the construction of the house. Everything was common, probably expensive, but plain, transitory, constructed to minimums. If Hotchkiss had built this lair he had done it with the intention of any day abandoning it. The entire house was disposable, a throwaway. The sink in the bathroom was fiberglass, the carpets industrial-type, an ugly pale-green tight twill, wall-to-wall, the same in every room, the door handles and bath fixtures not worth the slightest, serviceable just for the time being.

I walked along the hallway and peered into a few of the rooms. Each one was the same, large, with a seating area near one side or the other, ugly furniture in oppressively dull tones of beige and rust, faded earth tones. There was a light layer of dust on everything and bits of litter here and there.

At the end of the hall was a kitchen—again huge by ordinary standards—but furnished with appliances like the ones in the kitchen of a recreational vehicle. I realized how hungry I was. I hadn't eaten again for a day, maybe more. What was it about this whole trip that kept me from regular meals? I opened the refrigerator and was amazed. It was packed with the most succulent food. Pâtés, beautifully prepared salads, stacks of sandwiches, all apparently recently made, fresh fruits and juices. I took a sandwich and ate it. It was delicious—fresh lettuce and cucumbers with avocado and a slice of exotic, sharp cheese on the freshest and nuttiest bread. The odd thing was I could not help feeling as if I had stolen it, so inhospitable were the living conditions.

I noticed there were no plants, no greenery, no flowers or pictures of flowers. The walls were bare except for smudges around the light switches. Yet, the size of this whole house was so enormous, and its location so remote and difficult, it must have cost millions of dollars to construct and finish.

Out each window were sheer drops of fifty to a hundred

feet. The house was separate from each of the hilltops around it by twenty or thirty feet, so the isolation was complete.

I looked around the kitchen for a trash basket to throw away the sandwich wrapper, but didn't see one, so I threw it in the sink and continued my exploration. It did not appear anyone else was awake. I was halfway looking for the library Armando had mentioned; I could tell a lot by looking at his books. Instead I came to a great room with a sign above the door saying SUNSET ROOM. Inside was Armando himself, seated at a computer, still dressed in the silk bathrobe and slippers from the night before. Next to him was an empty bottle of brandy and he was smoking a Lucky Strike while he pecked with one finger at the keyboard in front of him.

At one end of the room was a wall-size picture window, looking across a gully to a neighboring hilltop twenty feet away. The soil outside was a brutal brownish-gray that I could see was matched by the skies, a flat, low overcast and light rain. There was no trace of flora, just a gathering mud rolling away across the bald hill.

Armando looked up as I walked in. "Well, you're up," he said, words a little thick. I gathered he was in his cups from the brandy. Either he was an alcoholic or he had been up all night—probably both. "I never got back to sleep, so I thought I would come and see what was happening in the planet's self-constructing neural net."

"I got up a few minutes ago. Neffie is still asleep. I got a sandwich from the kitchen. I hope you don't mind."

"Oh, is that all? Let me get you something else." He triggered an intercom next to him. "What would you like, breakfast?"

193

Though his speech slurred ever so slightly, he was lucid and alert, something beyond me and any booze I might have.

"I don't know, I . . ."

He spoke into the intercom.

"Tommy, bring a couple of bagels, some cream cheese and lox, and . . . let's see . . . a quart of orange juice and a pot of coffee. We're in the sunset room." He looked at me, smiled and took a long drag of the last of the Lucky Strike, which he stubbed out in an ashtray full of brother butts.

"Tommy will get you something. It'll be a minute."

Armando was seated at a folding table with an elaborate desktop computer on it. Around the room were other folding tables stacked with piles and piles of color copies, and along every wall, stuck to the drywall with pushpins, were hundreds of pictures, all pornography. I was intimidated. Armando knew that and enjoyed it. I was trying not to look. He saw me.

"Shocking, isn't it? The mind of a new media." He lit another Lucky. "But only shocking for a moment."

The stacks of papers on each of the tables turned out to be more pornographic pictures. Armando stood up.

"Here, don't be afraid. Look." He handed me a particularly graphic photo of a bound woman with several men around her having their way.

"What is this?" I asked, glancing at the photo, then laying it back down on the table next to the computer.

"Men at work," said Armando.

Tommy showed up at the door with the tray of food Armando had requested. He tapped lightly on the doorjamb to get our attention. Armando beckoned him in as he cleared a space from the pile of the photos on one of the tables, stacking the photos on the floor.

"Put it there. Thanks."

Tommy put the tray of food where Armando had instructed and left. Armando held up a Styrofoam plate of toasted bagels.

"Here," he said. "Eat."

I was still hungry, so I pulled a rickety folding chair up to the little table and made myself a bagel with lox and cream cheese—one of my least favorite foods, but these were delectable, the best I ever had.

"Is this what you do?" I asked between bites.

"By *this* you mean . . . ?" he waited for me to fill in the aposiopesis.

"Pornography. Do . . ."

"Not unless you call the phone company a pornographer because of obscene phone calls. I run Web sites, on the Internet. This is the stuff people post. I have nothing to do with it."

"You're an Internet service provider?"

"No, no. I started a Web site, that's all. A place where people can see what other people have posted, of themselves, of things they have. I started with a photographer, and when he found he got more hits by doing nudes, he started doing harder and harder stuff. I have ten sites now, all password-protected. Look."

He sat in front of the computer and pulled up a Web browser. Then he punched in a URL for someplace I didn't recognize.

"This site is in—well, I'm not going to tell you where it is—but it's not in the U.S."

The first page came up, simple graphics and a text description of what was inside, which was sex. The page had a telephone number to call for a password, which was good for twenty-four hours.

"You bring up the page on your browser, you get the number, call it, and get a password. Then you can go into the page and download whatever you want. On some of them I have a link to a bulletin board where you can upload as well. The telephone number is the international equivalent of a nine-hundred number—you know, where the caller pays? Each call is about two dollars to the caller. I keep a dollar forty and the phone company keeps sixty cents. Every week they send me a check."

"You don't make any of the content on the site?" I asked.

"Not one pixel. We make the home page describing the goods. That's it. The rest comes from the patrons."

"How many people sign on a day?"

"On all ten sites, eight-hundred thousand." He looked at me and smiled through another puff. It took a minute to sink in.

"Eight-hundred thousand? Wait a minute, that's . . ."

"A million-six. Roughly. Some days more. Some less."

My head reeled. More astronomical numbers.

"That's like . . . like . . ."

"It's not like anything. Not Disneyland. Not Home Shopping Network. Not the New York subway. It is a brave new world. I'm getting out of it."

"A million dollars a day is very . . . it's a lot," I said, idiotically.

"Not as much as you think. It seems big because I don't

do anything. But then, that's the secret, isn't it? Do as little as possible and make as much as you can.'' The smoke curled around his head, he flicked an ash into the ashtray, and leaned back in his swivel chair.

He was saying something I had heard many times before, usually from people who were trying to run a con game, losers with nowhere to go, trying to eke out a life. Except Armando was making over a million dollars a day trafficking in pornography and was getting his check from the phone company.

''This game is over, though. I'm moving on.''

I finished all the food, most of the orange juice—fresh— and some of the excellent coffee. Armando had not eaten any. He buzzed for Tommy, who showed up and cleared everything.

''Tommy, bring me another bottle of this.'' Armando held up the almost-empty brandy bottle for Tommy to see. He dug through some of the photos and produced a tin of Altoids, mint candy.

''I'm going into an Altoid, coffee, cigarettes, and brandy period. I can feel it. I couldn't get to sleep last night, which I was afraid of. If I get woken up inside of an hour after I go to sleep, I can't go back to sleep. I stayed up all night. I guess I'll stay up all night tonight as well.'' He stared at me, silent, intrusive. Then he said, ''I looked you up on the Net.'' More stare, deeper intrusion, waiting for a reaction. My eyebrows raised in spite of all my effort.

''You have quite a history. Not a great one, mind you. I thought you might be somebody really important, coming here with Neftoon Zamora and all, but you're an interesting 'also-ran.' '' He turned his head slightly to the side, his eyes never leaving mine, pushed the fingertip-size Lucky to his lips, took a drag, then blew the smoke from the corner of his mouth up and out toward the cottage cheese ceiling. He stubbed out the butt. All without once taking his eyes away. "Is the stuff I found true? Did you invent that cable thing, that music, what's it?"

He meant Music Television, MTV. It was a popular and successful cable television service. Clearly, he knew this.

"Everybody invented MTV. It's a running joke." I said.

"Yes, but you really did, didn't you? You're not joking. It's in the books."

"Well . . ." I hated this. There was a subtle, arrogant will at work, sliding up the power tree, looking for control, domination. My ego started into overdrive. Who was this jerk? What did he mean, an interesting "also-ran"?

"What's it worth?"

"MTV? I don't know. A lot."

"A lot?" he smirked. "He reached for the brandy and poured the dregs into a Flintstones' jelly glass. "I'd say a billion U.S. How much of that did you get?"

I hadn't gotten very much. I was paid well enough for the work I did. Perhaps I had come up with the basic idea, but other people had built the enterprise. They made all the money. What I received was peanuts by comparison.

"A lot." I said. I was in the grips of something terrible. I was defensive and afraid.

"You say *a lot* a lot. How much then?" The smirk widened into clear derision.

I was lying, protecting myself from this man's opinion. It was horrifying. What made me want to impress him, or to best him? Why was I falling backward? I had to stop myself, but I didn't know how.

"Plenty. If it's any of your business." A childish move. I drew myself to full mental height, and felt like a moron next to Armando. This was a goading, insidiously hateful man, pushing me back on my heels, making me stutter, explain myself, calling my very existence into question by his attitude of scorn.

"No, no, it's none of my business. I only wondered." He grinned, pleased with my obvious discomfort. "But . . ." he paused, took a sip of brandy, and his mouth curled in disdain. "If you are just a simple sideline player, a marginal, sort of meaningless . . . what? Artist? Business-man? I don't really know what you'd call what you do . . . then, how do you keep going? What gets you up in the morning, if it's going to be just another mediocre day, just one more failure of some kind?" The disdain faded into a mocking, malicious leer, then to a sincere and waiting ope-ness. I had never seen so many change-ups so fast. "How do you go on?"

What a question. It was ironic I should have any concerns about the opinions of this apparently lonely, greedy little man, hunched like a troll over his computer, brokering por-nographic picture-distribution services, but the question was at once so sarcastic and then again so pointed and genuine I was totally off balance.

"I don't know what you mean," I said.

"Bullshit. The question is how do people like you keep going? What drives you forward? Do you draw strength from your family, from your career, from your friends? What?

Because if that's what it is, then you're just an idiot. Somehow, though, I think you may be smart, and if it's something else, I want to know what it is. I really do." He had relaxed. The pointed attack on me subsided.

I would ordinarily resist this type of cynical and confused interrogation, but there was a strange quality about this man that made me stay with him, made me want to answer—perhaps not to defend myself anymore, but to explain things the way I saw them. The most important thing in my mind though was staying calm. Armando Hotchkiss was infuriating, and I instinctively knew better than to quarrel with him.

"My friends and my career are beyond your ability to comprehend, and I mean no offense . . . or defense, by this. But if you really want to know what keeps me going, I can give you some clues. It's a love of beauty, a love of life, to find activities to express that love and beauty completely, to live . . ."

"More bullshit. That's exactly what I thought you would say," he interrupted. "Let me ask you another question. Do you believe in God?"

"What difference does that make?" I thought of LittleHorse.

"Okay. Don't tell me. You know, people like you never get anywhere because you do not understand the importance of power. How it works, where it comes from, and how to get it. Popularity is power. That's the cheapest trick—a winning smile, good dinner parties—there is some power in that. Money is power. The real control of big money gets you a long way in this world. It doesn't even have to be your own money as long as you control it, but if it is, then your power is up an order of magnitude. Knowledge

200

is power. Do you know what I did in the sixties? When I was forty-three? I took the SAT's, the college-entrance exam. I made a perfect score. Perfect. I didn't miss one question. You know why I did that? Because I wanted to be sure I was not going to get passed by other people with more knowledge than me.''

"You seriously think making a perfect score on the general-entrance exams for American colleges and universities is a sign of real knowledge?'' I didn't deliberately infuse the words with stunned incredulity, but they were. Armando sneered.

"I don't think *anything* I don't think *seriously*. You'd do well to take a lesson from that,'' he growled.

Okay, I thought. Rich first. Smart second. A distant second, and in his case, also last. This was probably all there was to Armando Hotchkiss. I knew some smart, rich people, but I never knew a smart criminal, even though all the criminals I knew tested well, very well indeed. Armando might be sidestepping any criminal involvement with the pornography he was brokering. I'd be willing to bet he could even make a good case for the morality of pornography, but he was as crooked as the branch of a dead oak—bent, twisted. That was clear, so somewhere in all this, he was not as smart as he thought he was.

"If you have any two of those three—popularity, money, knowledge—you will have all the power you need. Any two. Me, I have all three, and I have needed them less and less as I have gotten older. You know why? Because power begets power. Now that I am getting ready to die, I have finally learned the secret of all power, a secret you will never know. Because, my boy, you see, talent is not power, skill is not power, trying to do the right thing is not power, and I'll tell you without question, beauty is not power. None of those things will bring you power, much less real money, and never will. In fact, you will lose what power you have because these things blind you so." He leaned back in the cheap swivel chair and smiled, satisfied. He lit another Lucky, took another long puff, and held it in.

Tommy came into the room and set a new bottle of brandy next to Armando. "Everything is ready. Whenever you wish, I can let them know," he said to Armando. Armando nodded as he hoisted the Flintstones' glass, sticky from all the earlier drinks, and filled it half-full with the booze.

"I know better than to offer you any of this, so you'll excuse me." He took a big gulp, devouring half of what he had poured.

"So you feel as if you have achieved all power?" I asked, honestly curious about what this man could be thinking.

"Oh, my son, my son. Why would you ask such a question unless you were dull. Of course not, of course not. I have never sought omnipotence. It's a fool's errand."

"Then what—three-quarter power?"

"Don't be cute. Think about this. What is the means of survival? Power over your environment. When the first men danced around the campfire, what were they doing? They were trying to control their experience, to make it rain, or stop raining, whatever. Why? To survive. Everything we do is to survive—not only this mortal life but whatever life there may be. I seek power not because I want to play with it, but because I must, because I am naturally selected to.

What do I do with it? I destroy everything that would endanger me.''

"Excuse me, Armando, but that is a perverted sense of natural selection. You know, there is a town called Welach . . .''

Time stopped. It was as if all the walls of Armando's castle had folded outward and down and we were left, only the two of us, in an open field, some huge, impossible space. I heard nothing, I felt nothing.

Armando stared at me as if his heart had stopped beating. All the muscles in his body froze. I knew at this instant why I had come to this place, Kweethu notwithstanding. A terror crept over me, then awe. All of the events since I had left Doc's focused on this one moment between me and Armando. I knew I must protect Welach from him at all cost, knew Armando and Welach were mortal enemies, that one would not survive in the presence of the other.

Then I felt what Neftoon Zamora must have felt when she stood in the circle of closing wolves and knew she must run directly towards Black Wolf. I was sure I had no choice but to confront and confuse this man and draw him away from any notions of Welach, a city I now understood was sacred, must never be exposed to even the slightest possibility of discovery by one such as Armando Hotchkiss. The taunting, mocking questions before had aroused my defenses, but I was helpless because of it, without clarity of purpose other than my own ego and vanity. That petulant resistance would provide little real protection, would instead create only a cycle of reactions leading to angrier and angrier exchange covering no new ground. It would not do here.

What I could see now perfectly was that Welach was a secret place, known only to me and the others who sanctified it. I could also see why the inhabitants of Welach kept the town so remote, so hidden. I felt firsthand the palpable and real commitment to the treasures of Welach. From here I saw even clearer the importance of Chuchen, the master city, governing by its quiet and gentle laughter, the simple lives of its children, the beat of its heart. No, Armando would have no chance of ever discovering from me anything about Welach. Because this time, I knew what to do, exactly how to handle him.

Armando was alert, prickly, every sense aware, a giant predatory cat upon its prey, ready to pounce. I tried to bypass the remark about Welach, but I knew he would return.

"Natural selection isn't about . . ."

"What about Welach?" he interrupted, slowly, carefully.

"What? Oh, Welach. Nothing, really. I was just . . ."

Armando shifted in his chair. With the turn of his head, a gesture so slight but so distinct, stopping me again, he sized me up, looking for a flank to attack, and said, "then . . ." He paused for an eternity. "Why did you bring it up?"

I had only one move, but it was a move I was sure would work. Because now I understood Armando, this artless man with his billions, this empty soul looking for a Welach to exploit, to enlist into his service of useless ideas, his perverted and shallow sense of natural selection. This man who would exploit the myths of creation for ticket sales, could be confused and lost in an instant, just as easily as Neftoon Zamora had jumped over Black Wolf. First, the run directly at him.

"I was thinking about some of the legends. I don't need to tell you, Welach, like Santa Claus, doesn't really exist."

Then the jump.

"They represent something, I guess." A pause as long as his. "Nobody is sure what." I watched him and grinned, blank, inscrutable.

Then, there it was. In a quandary, he flickered, ever so slightly, like a still candle flame caught in the wind from the wings of a wayward moth, a confusion passing over his face. I had him. Was I making sense? Was I being vague? Was I just stupid? He didn't know. Armando could hear the words, but he couldn't hear the spirit.

We both sailed off the cliff.

"I really was commenting on your ideas about natural selection, the survival of the fittest. You know Darwin never used that phrase?"

Armando put his hand to his chin, and rubbed his thumb and forefinger back and forth together across it, contemplating. Then, he squinted and gazed at me. Was I just some enchanted fool?

I gave him one last parting non sequitur, one last moment of empty-headedness, destroying even the pretense of knowledge of the existence of Welach. "It really is about survival. I had the best sandwich I ever had right from your kitchen," and with that, all notions of Welach vanished in Armando's conviction of my stupidity, the natural condition of the species.

He settled fully back into his chair and waved his hand in the air, dismissive. Yes, I was a fool. Probably not even enchanted.

"Well, so much for all this. You're obviously a nice man, stupid, but pleasant enough. I don't want to get in a discussion with you about evolution *or* sandwiches. You have too much to learn and I have too little you could grasp. And besides, I have other problems." Armando stood up. I stood with him.

"When are you leaving?" he asked me.

"As soon as everyone is up, I would think."

"Very good. The Justice Department is in a snit and have gone into their Waco mode. We all should move along as soon as possible." He made it clear he had no intention of talking to me any further, pushed the remainder of the pack of Luckies, in his robe pocket and shuffled out of the room, holding the brandy and the Flintstones' glass precariously among the fingers of one hand.

As he walked out of the room and out of sight, the strangest sensation came over me, a victory, but without the celebration. I had closed the door to Welach as fast as I had opened it. I felt relieved, happy Welach had become such a part of me I had instinctively known it must hide from the likes of Armando.

I thought about Welach, about being uncomfortable with the people, feeling LittleHorse was posing when I first met him, too perfect a sage, too perfect a wise man. I measured that against the feelings I had here in Armando's castle. Everything in the castle made sense, an unpleasant place to be sure, but it was consistent, it all fit together. Welach didn't fit, seemed impossible, but it was the best place I had ever been. Even my own insecurities and difficulties faded in the light that radiated from Welach into my thinking. Welach was not a mystery, but a secret. Armando's castle was no secret—indeed, was obvious, even predictable.

The computer screen caught my eye. It was still at the home page Armando had pulled up. There were pictures of women in salacious poses with buttons and icons next to them, all with the telephone number to call for the password. I looked around the room.

Now that Armando was gone—or more to the point, now that I was alone—I took time to look at the pictures carefully. After the initial shock of pornography wears off, it stops having much effect, like looking at the meat counter of a local market, after a while you forget these are pieces of dead animals. I didn't know why the pictures on the wall had been chosen. They seemed the same as the pictures in the piles: no better, no worse; no more graphic, no less. Then I saw the children.

They were not on the wall but were part of a pile on one of the tables. In all there must have been ten- or twenty-thousand pictures, color copies from a computer file, and this pile of child pornography appeared to contain at least a thousand. I recoiled, then picked one up. It was a nude picture of a young girl, probably eight, legs apart, smiling and looking directly at the camera. I didn't know what to think. I was horrified in one way and angered in another. I picked up the next one, then the next, until I had shuffled through perhaps a dozen. The shock never wore off, but I was overtaken with a curiosity about this subject, wondering who could possibly be interested in such things. Armando had called it the mind of a new media. Could this be right?

What I did understand was that I wanted to do something to destroy these pictures, Armando, his enterprise. I sat down at the computer and started hacking around, following a vague idea that if this was the main controlling computer, maybe I could shut them all down and ruin his empire. It was a dumb idea born of spy stories and the whole omniscient computer nonsense, but it seemed worth the try. I got through to the local operating system easy enough, a couple of keystrokes, then I went through to his other Web sites, but I couldn't get into their operating systems. He didn't have a system-operator status, at least not from here. After a few tries of some passwords, all of which were ''authorization failed,'' I looked around in the local hard drives. There was about five gigabytes of storage on one internal and one external hard drive, most of them graphics files. I was sure these could not have been the only files of the pictures I saw, but just for the hell of it, I erased them. Then as one last, serious, ''up yours'' I reformatted all his drives, erasing everything, operating systems and all.

It was silly. I was not ever going to do any permanent damage to Armando this way. I kept thinking about all the movies and novels where the good guy goes in and gets to the main computer and blows up the planet, but there was nothing like that here. I had only managed to erase his hard drives, probably little more than a nuisance, but it felt good and that counted for something. I heard a noise and stood up, walking away from the computer. I half-hoped it was Armando, so I could discover with him that his hard drives had been trashed and I could shake my head in amazement and commiseration about these darn computers and computer glitches. ''Maybe it was a virus, Armando.''

Instead, Gus came in the room. He looked worried, but not for his life anymore.

"Is Armando here?" he asked. At that moment I heard the sound of a helicopter and a jet. Out the window of the sunset room, Gus and I watched the A Star and the Gulfstream streak skyward. We both knew Armando was on one or the other.

"No," I said. "He left about fifteen or twenty minutes ago."

Gus actually wrung his hands in dismay.

"What is it?" I asked.

"I think there is some kind of problem outside." He turned and motioned for me to follow him down the hall, across an open atrium and then to a window that looked out over the road that came through the front gate. He was right. There was a big problem.

Down the hill, still outside the double antipersonnel fences, hundreds of agents were amassing. In the distance I could see several motor homes and a few-dozen cars parked tactically advantaged for a siege. Thirty of the agents were coming up the hill along the main road, M16's slung across their arms in front, all wearing Kevlar helmets and black bulletproof vests. They were walking on either side of one of the baby tanks the Justice Department seems fond of using in assaults on secure residences. I felt like a Branch Davidian.

"Have you seen Neffie?" I asked Gus.

He shook his head.

"We better get out of here," I said, not wanting to clarify my presence among stacks of pornography to an attorney general who had just lost his main prey. "I'm going to get Neffie. We'll meet you at . . . I don't know, try to get to the plane. Look for a back way." He nodded in agreement and ran off to look.

I ran down the hall to our room but Neffie was not there. I called her name and heard an answer filter through the kitchen. I raced toward it.

Outside, I heard the growl of the tank and the hum and sizzle of high-powered electrical wires as they were severed. The engine of the tank roared over the noise.

I ran in the kitchen and called Neffie's name again. This time the answer was clearer. She had walked into the sunset room as we had walked out. As I dashed back to the room I heard the front door cracking in two. The little paper-and-wood house was coming apart effortlessly with the approach of the Justice Department tank. Neffie was looking at the pictures on the wall.

"My god," she said. "Look at this."

"We have to get out of here. That's the Feds coming through the front door. This is the last place I want them to find us."

Neffie had walked to the computer and was looking at the screen. It said FINISHED FORMATTING DRIVE C: FORMAT ANOTHER? Y,N? She read it, then looked at me. "What's this?"

"Really Neffie, I don't want to get caught in here. I'll explain later." There was another loud crash, glass breaking, more fencing ripping up.

"Why don't we just invoke the self-destruct function on this? This whole house is wired to it and will blow up in ten minutes." She looked at me urgently.

"Self-destruct? It will? I, uh, I just erased every-thing . . ." I looked at Neffie, who was smiling.

"I'm just kidding, Nez. I see what you did. It was a good thing. Useless, as you may have guessed, but a good thing."

I really did love this woman; so at ease in the most unnerving situations, able to play around, to not get caught-up in the drama. I smiled, then in spite of myself I laughed, but not without the conscious thought: I'm standing here, laughing as the United States Justice Department, the same ones who—without the slightest hesitation—killed eighty people in Waco, Texas, are taking aim with a tank at the very spot I'm standing on.

"It was a little like letting the air out of his tires, I know, but that probably fits with his petty-criminal mentality, however much money he has."

"Oh, no. Armando Hotchkiss is not a petty criminal. He's the real thing, genuine evil. It's him and the ones like him that are our only real worries at Welach. He's come the closest to finding us."

"So . . . you do know him?"

"No. Know *of* him."

"And . . . what does he want with Welach?"

"Who knows? Maybe to expose us, to destroy our life outside the system he corrupts. Maybe to exploit us, put up a supermarket, a parking lot, start a new cable channel. But mostly just to prove he and his ideas are right, that Welach can't exist. In fact, doesn't, in his evolution."

I now saw why she had brought me here, felt the jubilation of my momentary defeat of Armando. I was going to tell her of the encounter, how I had protected Welach, and in so doing had moved it into the most secret place in my heart, all of which I now understood had been her intention.

211

I was going to tell her what I understood of the songs of Neftoon Zamora, of the miracle of Chuchen, of the legends she had told me. I was going to grab her and smother her with gratitude and kisses.

But the front door exploded, inward.

The halls of the house began to fill with burly men all shouting in their command voice, a studied way of shouting designed to intimidate. Unfortunately for me it always made me laugh. I thought they sounded ridiculous, but ridiculous or not they were all shouting, "Everyone in this house is under arrest. ATF. Stay where you are and raise your hands. ATF." Someone must have nudged command-voice number one because immediately following this instruction came command-voice number two shouting, "ATF. You are all under arrest. Lay down on the floor and cover the back of your head with your hands. ATF. Do it now! ATF." Nothing like conflicting instructions from someone with a gun to create nuclear-grade anxiety.

The only way out was through the plate-glass window that formed the back of the sunset room. If we could get through, jump to the neighboring hill, we might have a chance to get out of the area. At least we would not be caught in the midst of twenty years-to-life.

For whatever reason the first band of ATF had turned down another hall, away from us, but I knew it was only a second before the next wave would come in and head our way.

I picked up the folding chair and threw it at the window. The chair broke to pieces, the window only shook. I picked up the swivel chair Armando had been sitting in and threw it. It just bounced off. I heard the next bunch running through the door. It sounded like the tank was right in back of them. The clatter of their boots rumbled, muffled by the junk carpet, like crates of apples being poured onto a marble floor. Neffie was standing beside me, watching the door. I reached in my pocket and nervously fingered the leather bag LittleHorse had given me. As I shook it, the stone fell out in my hand, a stone the size of a walnut, a stone suddenly with the weight of a meteorite.

I hurled it at the window with all my might. It must have hit the tension point of the glass, because the window shattered like the safety glass in a car, first turning white with millions of tiny scars, then falling out of the window frame into the gully outside, leaving a perfectly square, perfectly open hole.

Outside the drizzle and fog were completing their own assault on the compound. The day had closed down like a bad business, leaving only the murky traces of a dismal sky, the inside of a coffin. I stood there, hesitant, uncertain, thinking of the gorge between the window and the neighboring hilltop. What if the men with the automatic rifles were out there as well? What if the house was surrounded with them? What if I jumped into the void, somehow made it across the abyss, only to plop into a nest of angry young men with low-technology intelligence and high-technology ordnance?

Neffie stepped in front of me, pulling on my arm, urging me into a run. The closer I came to the window the more I could see into the chasm outside the window, deeper and deeper the closer I came. I gave a yell, a yell of terror and hope, and jumped. At that instant I felt Neffie's hand in the small of my back, pushing me like some primal force, a giant spring firing me from a cannon, and with almost no effort I

213

sailed over the pit and plowed headfirst into the hilltop, into the frosting of mud the drizzle had created on the dusty terrain, then rolled down the backside, away from the house.

The back of the hill was a shallow slope, and I rolled for a hundred feet before coming to a stop at the bottom. I was knocked out of breath and lay there, coming to my senses, for several seconds. I knew that even if they found me now, they could never prove I was in the house. I might have been wandering around out here, maybe prospecting, communing with nature. I could say almost anything I wanted now that I was away from the house. I sat up and looked around, alert for perimeter guards.

I looked for Neffie. She was nowhere in sight. Had she fallen into the gully between the window and the hill? I stayed on my knees and crawled back to the hilltop where I had landed. Impossibly, the fog became denser, closing around me, sometimes cutting my visibility to a few feet in front of me.

When I reached the top I could see back into the room through the shattered window. It was full of the serious men in black. They were looking at the pictures on the wall and in the piles around on the tables. I peered over the edge into the gorge below, but there was no Neffie. The mist cleared, then gathered, then cleared again, billows of occlusion. I leaned farther over the hilltop into the hole, but she was not there. I studied the room carefully. She was not inside. She was not in the room. She had not fallen in the gap. And she was not with me. As I sat hunkered behind the hill of freedom, I heard the sound of an airplane engine, a sound I was sure was the Beech. I stood up and ran full-speed toward the sound, the runway and maybe, I hoped, Neffie.

11

1 RAN DOWN THE SLOPE OF THE HILL TO THE LEVEL ground. As I rounded the bottom of the hill I could see I was at the end of the airstrip and the Bonanza was coming to the end of the taxiway, about to turn onto the runway and take off. From the hangar, blurred in the mist, I saw two jeeps driving at high speeds toward the aircraft. I didn't know whether I could make it to the plane, but made the decision to try and committed myself to it, sprinting to the edge of the pavement.

I was about fifteen feet behind the slow-taxiing plane as it pulled on to the runway.

I ran up behind it as Gus put in full power. In one jump I made it onto the right wing, hanging on to the handle above the door. When Gus felt the force of my lunge he powered back, but the Beech kept rolling. I jerked open the door and threw myself into the seat.

Gus looked at me, not recognizing me through all the mud. I pointed to the jeeps racing toward us.

''Go!'' I yelled.

Gus fire-walled the throttle and we began the takeoff roll. One of the jeeps turned onto the runway and began to head directly for the plane. At this point it was simply a question of numbers. Either the plane would be airborne and over the jeep before it got there or it would not. Heroics would not help. We were now in the arms of certain laws of aerodynamics. I stared at the airspeed indicator. The plane would lift off at around seventy knots. We were at thirty. The jeep was looming larger and larger as it raced down the runway. Then I could see the man standing in the back of the jeep, aiming an M16 at us.

Fifty-five knots. Gus began pulling back on the yoke, trying to get the little bird up. The nose came up slightly but there was no lift in the wings.

Sixty-five knots. The wheels were almost off. Seventy. We were flying, but only a few feet off the ground. The jeep was about twenty-five yards ahead. We would clear it easily, but what about the gun? To Gus's credit he banked the plane to a hard right, climbing as fast as he could. Because of the fog we were visible for only a few more seconds, then we were enclosed, everything outside the window of the plane a dark gray. I looked at the instruments again. We were still in a climbing right turn. I wanted to ask Gus if he could fly on instruments, but it was meaningless. If he could, we would be through the clouds in a matter of minutes. If he couldn't, we wouldn't.

He leveled the plane out and began a best rate of climb. I relaxed a little. A few more seconds and the gray outside the plane turned to white, then yellow; then we were through the cloud and into a clear, blue sky. I sighed and settled into the seat.

Gus trimmed up the plane for the climb and finally looked at me.

"Who are you?" he said, flatly.

"It's me, Nez. I was in the sunset room." No connection. Once more. "We met last night. With Neffie?"

Gus nodded, still bewildered, still cautious.

216

"You're not with the Justice Department?"

"No. I came with Neffie. I was the one that flew the plane. She was worried about Kweethu . . ." Finally it dawned on him.

"I told her the truth," he said.

"I think she believed you. Actually, I'm worried about Neffie. We both were getting out of Armando's the same way, from . . . from the study. But we got separated somehow."

"I'm not going back, if that's what you're wanting," Gus said, defensively.

It was what I wanted, but I knew it was impossible.

"I'm going to fly low until we get out of this area. I don't know if they got the tail number, or what, but all I want to do right now is get as far away from there as I can."

I nodded my understanding. "How did you get out?"

"The elevator. It goes down to the hangars. I would have left sooner, but I tried to put some fuel in. I only got about five gallons in the left tank before I heard them coming. We're going to have to stop. I'm trying to think where. The best would be an uncontrolled field with a gas station on it. You're a pilot?"

Gus was properly concerned with flying the plane and getting away, not the least interested in Neffie, me, or the preceding events. I nodded yes.

"Good. Get that sectional chart and see if you can find a gas stop we can get to in thirty minutes." He pointed to the backseat.

I had to find us fuel within thirty minutes, but at one-hundred-seventy-knots per hour that meant I could look in

217

a radius eighty miles around the airplane. In the sky, off-ramps are a hundred miles apart.

The only place I could find fuel was at Ely, but it was a controlled field. Even more troublesome, it was linked to Reno Center, which would most certainly have the tail number of the plane, if the ATF boys had managed to read it. I told Gus all this. Ely was really the only place to go.

"Then that's what we'll have to do," he said with a sigh of resignation.

As we leveled off at cruise altitude, I had a good look at Gus's pilot skills. He was not merely a good pilot, he was first-rate, smooth and confident.

"How long have you been flying?" I asked.

"Years," said Gus, and let it go at that. He was not interested in making small talk with me.

"I'm sorry about this mud," I said. "I fell down a hill"

Gus looked at me disdainfully, then back to the instruments. He didn't accept my apology.

"You'll have to get out at Ely," he said.

"Well . . ." I fumbled. "Harouk was waiting for us at your place."

"Harouk? You mean Li's little fairy?" Vitriol filled the plane waist-deep.

"I don't know about . . ." I said. "I mean, he was working with Li . . . far as I know." I was at a loss. Whatever was going on at the diner that made Gus come in shooting was nothing I knew about.

"That little bastard. I oughta break his neck." Gus's teeth were clenched.

"What did Harouk do?"

"Not Harouk. Harouk is just some prick Li kept around. I mean Li."

Gus was blustering. This was not a good conversation to be having with the pilot of the airplane in which I was a passenger. I looked for neutral ground.

"You think we'll be okay to Ely?" I asked.

"I think so," said Gus. "If that sonofabitch hadn't run off with all that cash I wouldn't be in this mess. Armando Hotchkiss is nobody you want to fool with. Does he think I can just make those lectures up?"

Gus was free-associating, but one thing was obvious, he felt damaged, treated unfairly, and I gathered, thought Li had caused it. It was also clear he was going to vent this all over me. If that was the case, I wanted to keep him calm, and provide relief without meddling, and do the best I could to convince Gus to let me stay with him until the center.

"Who . . . or what . . . is Armando?" I tried.

"One of the most incredible men I have ever known. Armando the Newt. That's his nickname. Did you know he made a perfect score on the SAT's when he was forty-three?"

"He told me. Armando the Newt? Like the salamanders that live in swimming-pool equipment?"

"No, like the creature that can live in fire . . . does live in fire. Mythological. Hell, Armando Hotchkiss is an impossibility. He's got an IQ of two hundred and something."

"So, he tests well. You're friends? Acquaintances?"

"He loaned me the money to build the center. One of my students introduced us about fifteen years ago. He was living in French Polynesia, bought an island that was sovereign, bought it from the croutons that lived there, some nose-boned natives, created a currency, and set up a safe haven for international money. Probably crime money, but Armando never got close enough to anything illegal to get caught, or always got out ahead of any trouble, as you've just seen. Had you ever met him before today?"

Croutons?

"No," I said.

"Armando likes anomalies. He always was saying that's how we learn the most, find the anomaly and chase it. Find the science behind it. Most people ignore aberrations as meaningless; they take the average, the consensus. The Newt always took the opposite. Find the hole, he said, find the flaw, follow it. That's where you find truth. And, he said, where you find truth you find an opportunity to make a buck."

I looked out the window and saw the ground. We were starting to get into cleared skies. Ely was just ahead. It was a good thing. The gas gauge read empty.

"You know what he's doing now? He's going into the trash business. He's going to put trash on a spaceship and send it to the sun. He says the next big energy source is fission, and we're going to need to do something with all the waste when it becomes our main energy source. Is that Ely?" He pointed to the town in front of us.

I nodded. "Yes. That's it. Fission?"

"Don't ask me." Gus was preparing the ship for descent and landing. "He's always so far ahead of everyone, I never know what he is talking about."

Gus was now thoroughly into the airplane, getting it

ready to land. The conversation was finished. I was glad we had gotten on to another subject besides Li and his recent larceny, or whatever had caused the hatred in Gus. I felt closer to the center by the minute.

So Armando was betting on fission as the next energy source, and since fission created so much waste—dangerous waste—he was going to set up waste-carrying spaceships. If all he did was make a deal to dispose of the nuclear waste already on the planet, he could make a fortune. And what better thing to do with it than put it in a remote-controlled rocket and shoot it into the sun? He was going to build a fleet of garbage rockets, trash blasters.

Would it work? Possibly. But I was certain there was something wrong in this, some child pornography in it some-where. On the face of it, it was pure Armando; find a need and fill it. Wasn't that the first law of entrepreneurship? I would have savored the irony of Armando, in flight from the Justice Department for kiddie porn, on his way to rid the planet of nuclear waste were it not for the fact I was sure this was a genuinely bad man.

Gus obviously didn't see it that way, even though it looked to me as if he might have spent the most terrifying time of his life in Armando's control. I could tell Gus had a few screws loose or maybe a couple of logic chips, even if he was a terrific pilot. His landing was textbook perfect, and as we taxied to the gas station at one side of the airport, the engine quit a little short of the fuel truck and we rolled to a stop, out of gas. I was watching every movement on the field, looking for a sign of the boys from any branch of the Justice Department. At this moment I was afraid of any official, from the FBI to Fish and Game.

"Great landing" I said. "I would like very much if I could continue on to the center. I don't know how. . . ."

Gus waved his hand; he had already decided. "All right, all right." I had passed muster.

The airport was quiet, not a sign of an official of any kind. Either they had not gotten the number, gotten it wrong, had forgotten to write it down, or who knows what. I always wondered about the idea the enforcement mechanism in society could break down because of the simple foibles of humans, like not bringing a pen to write with. Fragile, very fragile.

The refueling went without incident and we were quickly airborne again. Now Neffie took over the chambers of my mind. It was no use talking to Gus about her, so I closed my eyes and pretended to be asleep. I tried to think of any possible place she might have jumped, but I couldn't bring enough of the compound to mind to get anywhere with that. I hadn't heard any shots fired, so if she had been captured she was probably unhurt. And if she was captured, her presence there would be explainable. I finally came to the conclusion that the best thing for me to do was to wait till we got to the center and Harouk and I could make some calls. I felt a certain level of comfort she was not hurt or in danger, so I left it at that.

That was the conscious part. Inside a tremor had started and I began to shake. A sad and low despair was upon me, a whisper that let me know Neffie was gone forever. I had no feeling she was dead, but more that her time with me was over. Whatever man-woman connection there was, was lost; whatever magic she had brought was out of reach; whatever movement in the story of my life was stilled. The emotion was not grief, but it is the closest comparison I can make. I sank in the seat and silently the sorrow overtook me. I didn't want Gus to see this. Thankfully, he was content to fly without conversation, and for the rest of the trip to the center he did not ask for help in navigation.

When we arrived, Harouk and Monica were standing on the parking ramp outside the hangars. I had forgotten the mud that covered me, but Monica's look reminded me. Monica rushed to Gus and hugged him, Harouk stood next to me with a look of knowing that was disconcerting. Gus glared at Harouk for a second, but Monica interceded and pulled him away toward the center. She began questioning him urgently, but with the relief of someone whose worry has been suddenly and happily lifted. I bypassed any greeting to Harouk.

"Have you heard from Neffie?" I asked desperately.

Slowly Harouk shook his head. He was not surprised or concerned she was not with me.

"Why don't you get cleaned up. Let's get out of here. I'll tell you what I know when we have some time to talk," he said.

"Did you expect this? You act like . . ." Now I was unnerved.

"I never know what to expect from her. I'm not surprised she's not with you."

Monica walked back over to us after she had given Gus a loving push toward the compound. She brushed my shoulder and some dried mud fell off. She was upset too.

"You need to get cleaned up. There's a room with a shower you can use." She was near tears.

223

"Are you . . ." but Monica held up her hand to silence me.

"I'm okay. I have to adjust to the news. But I can do that. Follow me to your room, will you?"

The three of us walked together into the center and said nothing. Whatever had happened at the Newt's was devastating to Monica as well as to me, and neither of us could really explain it to the other. I knew Harouk was ready to leave, so I hurried with my shower. I gave Monica all my clothes, which she had graciously offered to clean.

While I stood in the shower and the water poured over me I finally let loose with the despair. For me, this was never a good idea, whatever my friends or dime-store psychiatrists said. It was not a purge or a catharsis, because to give over to grief and loneliness, to wail and wallow, reinforced both and has always left me worse than where they found me. Still, sometimes you can't help it, you can't stop yourself from being taken over, and that is what happened to me.

It was a feeling of loss, not of sorrow. I didn't think a terrible thing had happened to Neffie. Oddly, I had a sure sense she was well, but something had come into my life through the open door behind her, something more than a remarkable adventure, extraordinary people; more than a woman I wouldn't forget. It was a connection to a spirit—or more precisely—to spirit. An unspoken, unknowable thing between us had caused me to see and feel things in a new and unforetold way. The fear I had now, the loss I was feeling, was this awful idea maybe I would not have that any more. That—with the absence of Neffie's physical presence—I would lose her great spirit as well.

Like I say, I should not have given in to these maudlin

and useless ideas, this pitiful "poor me" crying, but I couldn't help myself. I turned the shower as hot as I could until the pain from the heat made me focus my attention somewhere beside the wandering of my mind.

As the steam rose and the water stung me, my time with Neffie started to come into focus. I will admit I did not know this, as I came out of the shower and sat on the edge of the bed that day, but I can see what was happening now. I had been given a taste of life without boundary, of life as spirit, of life as infinite. It was the music that brought me into this incredible world, now it was the spirit of that music I was starting to understand, and it lifted me up.

There was a light knock on the door. When I opened it, Harouk was standing there with my clothes folded in a pile. He looked at me for a second, checking my state of mind.

I looked down the hall and saw Gus walking up to us.

"You two leaving?" he asked.

"Soon as I'm dressed. Unless you need anything from us . . . I mean if we can help."

Gus looked at me and Harouk with pure disgust.

"Not unless you got twelve million bucks." He glared at Harouk. "Tell your faggot friend he destroyed everything I have. Someday, some way, I'm going to make him pay. When you two get out of here, I want you . . ."

Gus sounded like he was about to go off on some harangue, but Monica approached and he controlled himself.

"These may be a little damp. But I knew you were anxious, so I took them out of the dryer early. Where are you off to?"

Monica was sweet, pleasant to a fault. But it looked as

if her most impressive achievement was getting a rein on Gus, keeping him from self-destructing and taking thousands with him.

"I have to get back to New Mexico. My car is there," I said.

"Have a lovely trip. Gus, I think you need to talk to the kids." Monica smiled, dismissive.

I was momentarily overtaken with a tinge of concern for her.

"Thanks for everything, Monica. Will you be okay?" I made sure to include Gus with my eyes in the word *you*.

"We'll be fine," she said, grabbing Gus's hand in a *shut-up-I'll-do-the-talking* gesture. "I think it's time for us to try television. We really have to run. Good luck, boys." Monica reached over and gave me a peck on the cheek, a quiet connection between the two of us, of *thanks* and *we'll be okay*. I gave her a slight, encouraging smile. She and Gus walked off, hand in hand, down the hall.

In seconds Harouk and I were on the road. I was driving the El Camino, since he told me as we got to the car he couldn't drive. It was twilight, another Southwestern sunset was upon us, this time to our back, so the mesas and sky ahead were sinking into the hues of evening as we saw only reflected light.

"So . . . tell me." I turned to Harouk to see his expression, then back to the road. He nodded and looked at the floor, drawing something from inside.

"She said she might not come back with you. She's done this before. She has an ability to get lost for long stretches of time. I thought she was going to leave when we got to the center, but I guess she wanted to find out something or do more.''

''And where did she go? She was right behind me when I was jumping out of this fifth-story window, then I never saw her again. Do you know where she is?''

''No idea. But Nez, she isn't who you think or what you think. If you could go back and reconstruct all the events that happened to you when she vanished, it would all be perfectly reasonable. Not as far-fetched as the old Saturday-morning serials, where you watch someone drive over a cliff in a ball of flame at the end of one episode, then find out they jumped from the car right before it crashed at the beginning of the next. But it would be something like that.

''And where she has gone, I can't tell you because I don't know. This is what I do know. Neffie has the gift of becoming what you need when you need it. Her insight is angelic, her wisdom is cosmic, and her laughter is . . . well . . . she only laughs when something is funny. If you never see her again, your life has been changed and you will never be the same for having known her. As it is written, 'A little leaven, leavens the whole loaf. Allah be praised.' ''

Harouk was saying almost exactly what I thought he would say, and it wasn't helping my sadness.

''If I never see her again? I . . .''

''But . . . but . . . be happy to know you will see her again. She'll pop up, except I have no idea when or where. You'll find her, or she'll find you. That's the way it is with Neffie.''

''How long have you known her?'' I asked.

''Long time. More important than the time we've been

together is what we shared. I think she's so special because of her time in Welach, because of LittleHorse and RD.''

''I was thinking of going back to Welach, maybe looking up LittleHorse, trying to find out more. Is that where Neffie usually goes after she does whatever she is off doing?''

''I don't know. Welach is where she was raised, but it isn't her home. LittleHorse and RD are her family; RD is her brother. But going back to Welach is not so easy and doesn't always get you what you want.''

Her brother. Now I did feel like the idiot Armando said I was. Could I go back and recapture the lost moments of love, love I gave away to pride and jealousy? No, of course not. This added to my depressed state. Harouk went on.

''LittleHorse told me once, 'Do not try to revisit the process of inspiration.' You can take that for what it's worth. The important thing is Neffie is okay. You can be sure of that, and you can be sure she meant everything she said and did. You'll never lose any of that. Do you like malted-milk balls?''

''No, my least favorite candy,'' I said.

''When we get to the service station, will you stop so I can get some? It's all I've been thinking about for hours.''

We could not see the service station yet, but the glow reached into the sky across the horizon. It was orange, like the glow from the big sodium lights surrounding Armando the Newt's house-trailer fortress. I was happy to stop—we would have to stop for gas anyway—but this time I wasn't getting out of the car for any reason other than to fill-up.

I turned on the lights of the El Camino. I was sure we would drive the rest of the night, there would be no sense in stopping. I didn't know what to think of Harouk's information about Neffie, about going back to Welach. I liked Harouk, but didn't know him as anyone I could trust. I didn't know him at all, but he seemed to know a lot about me and Neffie.

Over the next rise the service station appeared, sprawled across the desert, a monster clacking and clicking in the night, hosting swarms of moths and other desert insects with its powerful yellow lights, hundreds of fiery eyes shining, incandescent, consuming. An inert yet undead beast devouring, consuming all. Malted-milk balls indeed.

12

I STOOD IN THE GLOAMING, POURING GAS INTO THE EL
Camino, while Harouk bounced around inside the service
station. For some reason, he was content to be ingested by
the beast, like Jonah in the whale, secure in the conviction
he would be regurgitated to the shores of his own reality in
time to get back in the car and back on the road. I was
happy the gas pumps were for credit cards so I didn't have
to go inside. I had just the opposite conviction.

While I stood waiting for the tank to fill, I pulled the
leather bag from my pants pocket as well as the silver–dollar-
size coin from my watch pocket. In the bag was a key and
seventy-five cents in quarters. I looked at the strange markings on the coin LittleHorse had sent me. It made no sense.

Harouk bounded from the front door like a child from
a ride at Disneyland. He was gulping malted-milk balls and
holding out a brown sack for me.

"Here. I got this for you," he said.

In the sack was an air freshener for a car and a necktie
with a picture of a cow repeated up and down the front. I
smiled.

"Thanks." I held up the air freshener, the perfect
service-station souvenir.

On the road again we were enclosed by the night, riding
our beam of headlights into the countryside.

"Are you a Muslim?" I asked Harouk.

"Yes and no. I am in spirit, but I have no home in the Nation of Islam, any more than I do in Christianity . . . or any religion I know of."

In a few hours we made it to Glenwood, gateway to the catwalk. From here I had no idea how to get to the cars. Harouk had fallen asleep and was dreaming of malted-milk land. I hated to wake him.

"Harouk." I shook him after I stopped the car outside of the Blue Front. "Harouk. We're in Glenwood. Now what?"

He was groggy as he lifted his head up above the window and looked around.

"Go to the Welach parking lot, where the cars are."

"I have no idea where that is," I told him.

"You don't?" This woke him up. "Neither do I. I thought you were paying attention when we drove out."

The little town of Glenwood was closed tight; it was well after midnight. I didn't imagine we could get a room.

"I was, but I don't know where to go from here. We didn't come this way." I got out of the car in disgust and looked up and down the road. No lights were on, the gas station was closed, the guest ranch next to the Blue Front was dark. Harouk got out and stood next to me. Everything was silent. "I think it's north of here, but . . ." I looked at Harouk.

"We could sleep in the car," he said.

"What good is sleep going to do? Am I going to go to sleep and magically wake up and know where the cars are parked? If I go to sleep stupid, I wake up stupid. If we go to sleep here we wake up here."

Harouk gave me a *my-aren't-we-bitchy* look. I felt like punching him.

"What?" I hissed. "You think I'm being unreasonable?"

At that moment the street was lit by an approaching car. The lights roamed over the face of the buildings until the vehicle came into view. It was a police cruiser.

It drove by without seeming to notice, then a quarter of a mile down the road made a U-turn and came back. As it approached the red lights came on, bleating strobes of red in the still, night air.

The car sat a few feet from us, lights shining, making Harouk and me grimace, holding our hands above our eyes. Then a spotlight blinded us for a few seconds, and went off along with the strobes and all the other lights on the car, leaving only the dark. The door of the cruiser opened, the dome light illuminating RD as he stepped out.

"Hey," he said, walking up slowly. "When did you get in?"

I looked at the name tag on his chest. It said Carlos Reyes. I was confused. I stared at the officer for a long time, then said, "RD?"

Officer Carlos Reyes nodded yes.

"This is my life in the outer world. Neffie gone?"

He aimed the question at Harouk, sure of the answer, but verifying it.

"Yeah. I haven't seen her since . . . we went to this place, it was in Nevada."

"Okay," said RD. "Follow me."

Runs Deep was huge, shoulders like a block of stone and over six-feet-six. He had all the actions and movements of a policeman. In the uniform he was formidable, so daunting a figure I didn't want to get near him.

RD got back in the cruiser and we followed him. After a few miles we came to a dirt road and I recognized it as the one that led to the place we had left the cars.

A few more miles up the road and we came to the little farmhouse, the sacred Indian land barrier to the casual hiker. Behind the farmhouse, farther up the dirt road, we came to the clearing. There was my car and Neffie's bike. The sight of the bike made my heart beat faster. RD parked and directed us over to a space.

Harouk and I unfolded from the El Camino. RD walked over, reached in the door of the car and took the keys, put them in his pocket, and stood, saying nothing.

I walked over to my car and checked inside. Everything was there: camping gear, road-food wrappers, luggage.

Harouk and RD were standing shoulder-to-shoulder now, watching me. I was confused. I looked at them, then the El Camino, then around the clearing. The two of them were saying nothing. It was as if they were in a club and I wasn't a member, that my time was up, the next person wanted my seat. I had my ride, now the time had come for me to go back to the fairgrounds and find something else to do. But all of the surprises were not over yet. RD walked toward me.

"Neffie wanted you to have this. She asked me to help you get it out of here." He held out a slip of paper, folded, with the markings of an official document. I opened it and read it. It was the title to the motorcycle, registered in the name of Miranda Clank and signed over to me on the transfer-of-ownership line.

I drew in a deep breath and let it out. I was starting to shake again. Is this what it is like to be drummed-out of the corps? To be driven from the herd? Do they give you enough to get along on the outside, a few relics and mementos of your past life among the chosen, and then send you into the void? I looked at the ground, then back to RD, then to the Harley.

I could refuse to take it. To not let the final chapter close. RD was unblinking, Mount Rushmore. Harouk had jumped in the cruiser and was eating the last of his candy.

"You're her brother?" I asked.

RD nodded.

"Will you see her?"

"She comes and goes."

Should I leave a message? What would I say? "I had a great time, please stay in touch, oh, by the way, you changed my life." So, I did what so many of us do in times like these: housework, bookkeeping, hair-and-makeup.

"How will I get this out of here?" I asked, pointing to the bike.

"If you stay overnight, I'll help you get a trailer in the morning." RD looked to the farmhouse.

"I can stay there?"

RD nodded.

"Okay. Okay. Then, yeah, I'll do that."

RD said nothing more and turned toward his car. In a few seconds the headlights sliced through the skies, glanced off the trees and were gone. I was motionless for a long while and at last sank to the ground where I had been standing, and sat cross-legged underneath heavens. On one side was the little adobe house, on the other my car and Neffie's jade-green Harley. In between were the mesas and the land, the black trees and the purple sky, the murmuring wind and the chuckling animals. The warm air settled around me and I could smell the water from the mountain streams as it seeped through the sands and settled in the wells.

A coyote yipped at the moon and was answered by a distant cry. I lay backwards and stretched out, across the dirt and grass, into the open space on either side of me, into the wilderness beyond, into my broken heart. The tears began to roll from the sides of my eyes, into my ears and onto the ground. My chest began to heave in great sobs until I was out of breath, and like a tired child I turned to the arms of my mother, spent. Across the night sky I began to see dozens of shooting stars, chasing each other around the supernal playground, the play of the young, delighted, care-free, a game of tag where no one is "it." Slowly my sorrow-racked body slid into sleep, into surcease from the encroaching weary world. For a few hours, at least, I would wander my dreams, wait until the morning, start with a new day the life that awaited me, tend to the new motorcycle.

I woke several hours later to the first light of dawn and sat up, creaky, aching from the hard ground. I was still tired, drained of energy. I made my way to the little adobe and went inside.

It was modest; three rooms, one with a bed. The bed was fresh and smelled of new-mown hay, of recently-woven thread from newly-spun yarn. I lay down and went to sleep again, exhausted. This time, in the early-morning hours, I began to dream. Neffie and I were walking in a city park. All around children were playing, and when they saw her they ran to her and grabbed her around the legs, squealing with joy, a repetition of the scene at Kweethu's. Neffie stroked their hair and patted their backs and shoulders. The children grabbed the fingers of each of her hands and pulled her to the ground so she could sit with them, and once seated they crawled over her, positioning themselves along her arms, in her lap. Somehow she held them all. The children wanted a story, and this is the story she told them.

Once, in a far-away land, lived a handsome man and a lovely woman. Together they roamed the land and discovered many things. One day, while the sun was shining and the sky was clear, a great bird flew to them, carrying in its beak a jewel with all the colors of life in it. The bird dropped this jewel at the foot of the woman, who picked it up and wove it into a belt she was making for the man, a belt made of fibers of wool and strands of gold. The woman placed the jewel in the center of the front of the belt. At this, the bird flew away. When the man saw the belt he was overjoyed and put it on at once.

That night, when the man and the woman were swimming in a beautiful lagoon outside their home, a great fish was drawn to the light from the jewel and swam up from the ocean deeps to bargain.

"Give me the jewel" he said, "and I will teach you the secret of all life."

But the man and the woman said *no*. "What we will do is let you use the jewel for a light back to your home."

"In that case," said the fish, "I will only tell you some of the secrets I know."

Thus, they agreed.

The fish said, "In life, only the good survive. In love, only the strong."

237

But instead of giving the fish the jewel to see by, the man and the woman said, "This is no secret. Go back to the depths of the sea, there, live in your world. This jewel can never be of any use to you, for it only shines by reflected light".

At this story all the children cheered with glee. Then Neffie stood up from the children and walked over to me. She was carrying a plate of corn tortillas. She held them under my nose and I slowly awoke to see the face of Kwee-thu standing over my bed. I sat up suddenly.

"RD says you want breakfast. I made these. I am making some beans with chili."

She laid a plate of tortillas on the table next to the bed. I took one and ate it. It was delicious. Once again, I thought about how my food intake had become so strange in the last week. It seems as if I only got food when I was starving. I heard Kweethu banging around in the kitchen. I got up and went to a bowl of water on a stand and rubbed my face and hands, then shook the sleep from my eyes and went into the kitchen.

"You're Kweethu?" I asked.

She nodded. She had put on a pot of water to boil.

"Runs Deep will be here soon with a trailer for your new motorbike," she said. "He wanted me to feed you first."

"We went looking for you, did you know that?" I asked her.

"For me? Why? I was playing cards. Why did you want me?"

"Neffie thought you were kidnapped."

Kweethu waved this remark away with her hand. "That

is too stupid for words. She knows I cannot be kidnapped. Where did she take you?''

Take me? Kweethu was thinking something different than what I was telling her.

''We went to Nevada.''

''Oh. Las Vegas. I want to go there sometime,'' Kwee-thu said, brightening. ''They have many games there.'' She stirred the pot. ''Did you like it?''

''No, we didn't go to Las Vegas. . . .''

''Oh, that's too bad. Next time I hope you get there.''

Two cars drove up outside and I heard the rattle of an empty trailer. I walked to the door and looked out. It was RD, in civilian clothes in a truck pulling the trailer, and Harouk and Li in a car. The three of them got out and stood around the trailer hitch, studying it. I went out to join them. My face must have shown how surprised I was to see Li.

''This will fit on your car,'' RD said as he unhitched the trailer and sat it on the ground. ''You'll have to back it over here, though.'' I hurried to my car and drove it to the spot where the trailer was as RD pulled his truck out of the way. I got out of the car and walked to the back while RD mus-cled the trailer into position and hooked it on.

''I didn't expect to see you again,'' I said to Harouk, but I loaded the statement to mean Li as well.

''What, and not say good-bye?''

''He wouldn't leave without seeing you first,'' Li said.

''And where are you going?'' I asked as RD walked up to join us.

Li and Harouk looked at each other, then to me. Li spoke. ''Maybe New Orleans. Maybe Vegas.''

''Li says Vegas is the fastest-growing city in America.''

"I've heard that," I said.

"But what you don't know," said Li, "is that the new major corridor of commerce will be from Las Vegas to Tijuana. Mexico is the coming gateway to the Pacific. Lots of opportunities there. We're going to set up somewhere between those two."

"Or New Orleans?" I said, needling Harouk, since it was clear Li had no intention of going to New Orleans.

"Yes. Yes. Maybe there." Li was scrambling.

"Li has some good ideas," said Harouk, defusing the bomb I had lit.

"Let's get the bike on the trailer." RD brought us to the task at hand.

The three of us wrestled the big bike up into position and tied it down. It would sit like that until I got where I was going. Wherever that might be. The thought must have been visible.

"Where are you going?" asked Li.

"I was thinking of staying around here. I saw some places on the high road to Taos that looked interesting. I might settle out here. Give me some time to look for Chuchen."

At this, all three of the men looked at each other, a shared knowledge.

"Won't find Chuchen, Nez," Harouk said. "Almost as hard as finding Welach again. Wouldn't waste too much time on that."

"Neffie said she found some signs," I said, putting a few more touches on tying down the bike.

"You will too," Harouk said. "But signs of Chuchen, and Chuchen itself—two different things."

"You're ready," said RD. "I have to go."

"Oh. Wait" I said. I squatted down and passed my hand over the earth, feeling for a stone. I dug a small rock the same size as the one LittleHorse had given me from the soil and stood up. "Give this to LittleHorse when you see him." I held up the rock, the key, and the seventy-five cents. "Tell him I had to throw the magic rock he gave me but I replaced it with this one. It worked exactly like he said."

I dropped everything into RD's open hand. "I'm keeping the leather bag. I think he meant for me to."

RD nodded his agreement, then unexpectedly he closed his other hand on top of mine and gave a gentle squeeze. There was real affection in his eyes and even a little respect. "I had my doubts," he said. "Not Neffie. She never worried. She said you reminded her of someone she knew, another musician. She was right. She usually is. I'll give all this to LittleHorse."

He had said all he would. He walked to his truck and drove away.

"We'll be leaving too," said Harouk. "You're a good guy, Nez. I wish you well." Harouk embraced me with a genuine warmth. "Who knows, maybe our paths will cross again."

Li extended his hand and I shook it.

"Sorry you got mixed up in all this," Li said. "Maybe next time I can keep everything going. This time I didn't do such a good job of making it work."

He and Harouk drove down the road, a wispy trail of dust waving their last good-byes, then vanishing into the air.

I examined the motorcycle trailer and hitch once more for good measure as Kweethu came from the house with a hot bowl of beans and some fresh tortillas. I sat on the edge

of the trailer eating them, scooping the beans with the tortillas.

Kweethu went back near the house and began pulling
some weeds around the base of the adobe. I heard footsteps
and turned to see a young man and woman walking up the
trail. I said nothing as they approached, but Kweethu stood
up and began to walk toward them, calling out before they
were even in the yard.

"No hiking here. This is Indian land. No hiking. Please
leave." She was tough, shrill, and deterring. The two kids
stopped, looking at each other.

"It says on this map . . ." the girl started.

"I don't care what it says on the map. This is private
Indian land. Sacred. White man's map means nothing here.
Go away. Now."

The hikers looked at each other again, agreed they didn't
want the hassle, and turned around, plodding back the way
they came.

Kweethu went back to her gardening.

"You're tough," I said to Kweethu after a minute.

"I know. These kids, they should be working. They
don't know anything. Can't just walk in here like that. Soon
all these white kids come around. Life becomes miserable."

I finished the beans.

"Thanks for breakfast," I said, but Kweethu did not
respond.

"I'm going to be going now." Still no response.

"Do you think you might see Neffie?" I asked.

Kweethu stood up and turned to me.

"You should forget about her," she said, as she walked
to me. When she was close she looked up at me, her wrin-

kled brown face shining in the new sun, her eyes laughing from behind the puppy-dog folds of skin surrounding them. Kweethu was less than five-feet tall, weathered, gray hair wrapped around her head. "One day she might look like me, then what would you do?" She smiled a questioning smile, raising her brows lightly.

"I think that would be fine, Kweethu. I think you're beautiful."

She opened her mouth into a wide grin. One of her lower teeth was gone. She studied my face, looking deep into my heart. "No," she said. "Neftoon Zamora will always be the same. She will never change. Neftoon Zamora is our home." She patted one hand over her heart.

I could see Kweethu knew more than she had said. I wanted to pursue this, but there was a shield she put up between us. Like the hikers, I was allowed to go no further. I thought of the coin LittleHorse had given me and pulled it from my watch pocket. I held it out to Kweethu.

"Do you know what this means?" I asked.

"Where did you get this? This is from Welach." She took the coin from me and examined it, looking for authenticity.

"LittleHorse. But I can't read the writing."

"It's too much to tell. The people of Welach carry them. They are the laws of life. It says there is only one spirit and there is nothing but spirit. But this can mean nothing to you. It is only for those in Welach." She handed the coin back.

"This spirit," I went on. "Is this spirit good?"

"Only good," she said. "But why ask these things? They are nothing to you. Only the tales of some old Indians."

If I could have told her what went through my mind at

that instant she might have told me more. But I was full, full of food and full of my adventure. She was right, I could hold no more now. The sayings on the little coin were only that, sayings. These last few days were mixed in my mind, a blur of gibberish and gratitude. It was true. I could make nothing of what she was saying.

"This is a pretty motorbike" Kweethu said. "Do you ride it well?"

"I can ride. Yeah. I can ride fairly well," I said.

"This was Neffie's. She gave it to you, right?"

I nodded my head.

"Could she ride it well?" Kweethu looked for my answer, an answer she already knew.

"Oh, yes," I said. "She could ride it very well."

"That is what I heard. Be careful on it. Don't fall down." Kweethu walked away from me and the bike, back into the adobe. The screen door slammed behind her.

I sat in my car for a second, taking one last long look around. I started up the engine and instantly the sound of the blues filled the air, blasting. The radio was on loud, the tape still in the player. The songs of Neftoon Zamora sang out into the day. As I bumped down the narrow road, away from the little house guarding the entrance to the sacred city of Welach, I noticed for the first time that the color of the sand in this road was exactly the same as Neffie's hair. The road twisted, turned, and waved as it flowed in front of the car, as it wound to the horizon.

Like her hair, it was the defining feature of the landscape. The low pines and distant mesas, the high sky with angel-hair cirrus strands painted across it, the shining sun bathing

the land in warmth—all were drawn into unity by this sig-
nature, this path in front of me, long and sandy.

I heard the soulful, scratchy, neither-man-nor-woman
voice of Jefferson Washington pour the words of Neftoon
Zamora deep into my soul. "You got to trust the pilot when
you get on the plane."